"Mmm." She sighed as his thumbs circled the base of her neck. **"Right there."**

"There?" At her positive nod, his hands made their way under the sweetheart neckline of her blouse, sliding his fingers up and down her neck and shoulders.

The touch of his flesh against hers almost sent him over the edge into madness, but he maintained his sanity somehow; however, when she purred deep in her throat and softly spoke his name on a serrated sigh of desire— that was his undoing.

Swiveling her chair around, he pulled her up out of her seat until her soft body was pressed against his solid one, and without giving her or himself time to think, he fused his lips to hers. Her mouth was opened in a half gasp of surprise, which he took full advantage of, slipping his seeking tongue out of her white teeth in search of

Oh, my Lo properly, was even better rasn't an option. Tast mouth was his only objective out that mission with a vengeance.

Books by Judy Lynn Hubbard

Harlequin Kimani Romance

These Arms of Mine
Our First Dance
Our First Kiss
Our First Embrace

JUDY LYNN HUBBARD

is a Texas native who has always been an avid reader—particularly of romance. Judy loves well-written, engaging stories with characters she can identify with, empathize with and root for. When writing, she honestly can't wait to see what happens next; she knows if she feels that way, she's created characters and a story that readers will thoroughly enjoy, and that's her ultimate goal.

OUR FIRST Embrace

JUDY LYNN HUBBARD

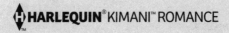

HARLEQUIN® KIMANI™ ROMANCE

Recycling programs
for this product may
not exist in your area.

ISBN-13: 978-0-373-86347-1

OUR FIRST EMBRACE

Printed in U.S.A.

www.Harlequin.com

Dear Reader,

Our First Embrace was a story that simply took me away, and I hope it does the same for you. There was so much I wanted to tell, but so few pages I had to tell it in. More than once, I bemoaned my word count limitations.

This book was supposed to be the third and final installment in the Carter sibling trilogy. However, as I wrote *Our First Embrace,* the character of Victor James (Alexander's brother) really stood out for me. I think he's worthy of his own book. Is Monique (Nicole's friend and coworker) the woman for Victor, or is there someone else waiting in the wings? Stay tuned to find out.

In the meantime, cuddle up with Nicole and Alexander as they search for their happily ever after. I hope you enjoy *Our First Embrace.*

As always, thank you for your continued support, and happy reading!

Judy

www.JudyLynnHubbard.com

Chapter 1

Paris in the springtime! Native New Yorker, twenty-five-year-old Nicole Carter, couldn't believe she was finally in France.

It was a beautiful Monday morning with plenty of sunshine. The temperature was a cool forty-two degrees, and she didn't bother to fasten her light jacket as she walked along the sidewalk, passing various brightly colored cafés that beckoned her to stop; however, she resisted. The last thing she needed was to be late for her first day.

She was in enough trouble already—arriving a week later than scheduled so she could attend her brother's wedding in New York. Alexander James, her new boss, hadn't been too happy about her requested delay, and she prayed he wouldn't hold it against her.

Nicole halted in front of a six-story stone building that housed Alexander's Fashion House. She stood outside for a few seconds smiling at the edifice before opening the glass door and walking inside. Opulent surroundings greeted her—black-and-white marble floors, tapestry chairs and expensive artwork. Everything about Alexander's screamed class.

She approached the security booth, and after receiving her badge was directed to the sixth floor. Upon exiting the elevator, Nicole checked in with the receptionist, who showed her to Alexander James's office. She paused long enough to take several calming breaths before rapping lightly on the closed wooden door and plastering a smile on her face. Then she opened the door and went inside.

The first thing she noticed was how large and spacious the office was. With its heavy wood-and-leather furniture, it had definitely been decorated for a man by a man. The hardwood floor shone. Huge windows occupied the entire back wall, allowing a multitude of light to stream in and soften the dark decor.

The second thing she noticed was the imposing man rising from behind a massive mahogany desk as she entered. He had to be over six feet—definitely the master of his domain. Alexander James's photos didn't begin to do him justice.

He was dressed casually in a navy blazer, white shirt, no tie and navy slacks. He wore his dark brown hair slightly long and curly. His skin tone was much lighter than hers; the café-au-lait complexion reflected his heritage, his mother being European and his father African-American. It was his hazel eyes flecked with gold that really drew Nicole in—even though at the moment they were dancing with displeasure and directed squarely at her.

"Welcome to Paris, Miss Carter." Alexander's deep voice caressed her skin, and prickles shot up her arm as he briefly clasped her small hand in his large one.

"Thank you." She sat in the seat he motioned to in front of his desk, and he resumed his seat behind it.

"Did you have a nice flight?"

"Yes." She crossed her legs, resting her hands in her lap. "Thank you for asking."

"Is your hotel satisfactory?"

"It's beautiful," she assured. Calling her temporary home, the art deco–inspired Lutetia, a hotel seemed insulting.

"Good." He nodded. "You should be comfortable there until you can find more permanent quarters."

"I plan to look for something this weekend."

"I expected you to have a place lined up before arriving."

"I meant to, but…" Her voice trailed off.

"But time got away from you."

Her shoulders stiffened at his slightly accusatory tone. She met his cool gaze with one of her own. So this was the way it was going to be? She sighed inwardly.

"Life happens, Mr. James," she tightly informed him.

"Prudent planning is worth its weight in gold, Miss Carter." He folded his arms across his broad chest. "Wouldn't you agree?"

"Whenever possible." She silently counted to ten and reminded herself he was her new boss, and she wanted this job.

Alexander remained silent while his eyes studied her from head to toe. She reminded him of a porcelain doll. Her shapely figure was accentuated by her crisp and professional black pantsuit. Her short tapered hairstyle perfectly framed her heart-shaped face, and her deep brown eyes were very expressive—at the moment, tinged with frustration. She was a beautiful woman, a fact he was angry at himself for noticing. She was his employee; she was here to work, and work she would!

"We're having an in-house spring show at the end of next month and then a big yearly show at the end of August." He sat back in his plush leather chair and tapped his desktop with his fingers. "You're already a week behind."

"You'll find I'm not afraid of hard work, Mr. James," she promised.

"For your sake I hope not." He smiled without humor. "You have a lot of catching up to do."

"For goodness' sake, I'm only a week late—not a month," she snapped.

"A lot of work can be lost in a week," he informed tightly. "I don't like wasting time."

"Neither do I, Mr. James."

"Really?" He raised a skeptical eyebrow. "Actions speak louder than words, Miss Carter. I hope I didn't make a mistake hiring you."

She visibly bristled at his insinuation. "You didn't."

"Time will tell." He wasn't at all convinced. "I'm going to start you on the Bettina line. I trust you had time to familiarize yourself with the information packet I sent you."

"Yes, I did," she assured him. "Bettina is your casual and affordable chic line catering to the twenty to twenty-five age range."

When he showed no signs of being impressed with her answer, she snapped open her portfolio and handed him five sketches.

"What are these?"

"Sketches I took the liberty of preparing while I kept you waiting." Her voice was tinged with sarcasm, prompting him to raise one of his eyebrows.

Without a word, he flipped from one sketch to the next, purposefully keeping his expression unreadable. They were good, very good, but he wouldn't give her the satisfaction of knowing that yet. He needed to see what she was made of—find out if she possessed the dedication and stamina to handle the demands he would place on her.

He wasn't running a nursery, and he had no intention

of coddling her or any of his employees. Her actions made him question his choosing her for the coveted position with his company, and he didn't like second-guessing himself. She'd cut it or she'd be out on the door before she could blink her pretty brown eyes. After a cursory exploration of the designs, he placed them on his desk and stared at her silently.

"Well?" She bristled under his cool scrutiny.

"It's nice to know you gave some thought to work while we waited for you to show up."

"What do you think of them?" She seemed to be fighting the urge to scream in frustration.

"They're adequate." He shrugged. "They could have been passable had you been here *on time.*"

He almost smiled when her eyes darkened angrily. "Mr. James, how many times…"

"I hope you had a nice time while you kept us waiting, Miss Carter, because I'm going to work you until you drop," he darkly promised, interrupting her tirade before it could begin.

"Give it your best shot, Mr. James." She picked up her sketches and replaced them in her portfolio.

He punched a button on his phone, "Jean, send in Monique." He stood and returned his attention to Nicole. "That'll be all, Miss Carter. Monique, one of my *dedicated* head designers, will show you to your workstation. If you need anything, let her know."

Right on cue, a rap sounded on his door, and it opened to admit Monique, a smiling, slender African-American woman who honed in on Nicole. She and Nicole were about the same height, though Monique was a couple of years older. Her long black hair was pulled away from her smiling face.

"Hi, Nicole. I'm Monique." She extended a hand, which Nicole shook. "Welcome to Alexander's."

"Thank you." Nicole smiled at her genuine welcome. "It's nice to meet you."

"You, too." Monique glanced at a stoic Alexander. "I'll show you around if the boss is done with you."

"We're through for now," Alex agreed, sitting back down behind his desk. "Thanks, Monique."

"Sure thing, boss." Monique opened the door and waited for her to gather her belongings. "Ready, Nicole?"

"More than." Nicole sighed and left the office. Alex watched them go, his eyes boring into her back.

She repressed the urge to stomp out of his office as she preceded Monique through the door. What an infuriating man! She sighed audibly once the door closed behind them.

Monique chuckled. "That bad, huh?"

"No, it was fine." At Monique's skeptical look she elaborated. "He is…" She paused, not sure if she was talking to a friend or a foe. "It was fine," she reiterated.

Monique laughed, linked her arm through Nicole's and pulled her away. "Oh, I'll bet!" She smiled and whispered conspiratorially, "You can trust me. I'm a fellow New Yorker."

"Really?" Nicole brightened at the mention of home.

"Mmm-hmm, born and raised. I transferred from Alexander's New York office five years ago. You're planning on transferring to that office after your six months here, right?"

"Yes," Nicole confirmed. Right now, she couldn't wait for that day to come. "Do you like it here?"

"I love it." Monique beamed. "You will, too. I promise."

"This is a fantastic opportunity for me. I plan to make the most of it."

"I'll help you any way I can," Monique promised. "I predict we're going to be good friends."

"I think so, too," Nicole agreed.

"Definitely," Monique assured. "How about some coffee before I show you to your station?"

"I'd love some." Nicole groaned gratefully, and Monique laughed.

"The break room is in here."

Monique led her into an attractive white room with rows of laminate tables and matching padded chairs. There was a full kitchen, including several refrigerators, microwaves and conventional ovens. Her eyes widened as Monique poured two cups of coffee not into Styrofoam, but into china cups.

"Very nice." Nicole took the offered cup from Monique.

"The boss believes in doing little things like this to keep us happy." Monique shrugged as they sat down at one of the tables. "He's really not bad once you get to know him."

"Time will tell." After adding cream and sugar, Nicole sipped her coffee and felt some of the tension leaving her. "He's upset because I'm late."

"You had a wedding to attend, right?"

"Yes." Nicole smiled fondly. "My brother's."

"Well, you couldn't miss that."

"No, I couldn't." Nicole sighed. "I wish Mr. James understood that."

"He'll get over it," Monique predicted. "Just wow him with your fabulous work ethic and tremendous talent."

"I'll try."

"You'll be fine, and like I said, I'll help you in any way I can."

"Thank you."

"You're welcome." Monique squeezed her hand and winked. "We New Yorkers have to stick together."

"Definitely." Nicole returned her smile, feeling at ease for the first time that morning.

* * *

Victor James entered his older brother's office without knocking. He chuckled at Alex's raised eyebrow as he plopped down on the edge of his desk.

"Hey bro, what's up?"

Alex frowned. "I'm trying to get some work done."

"Well, that's why I'm here." At his brother's confused stare, Victor reminded him, "You said your computer was, in your words, *acting squirrely.*"

"Oh, yeah." Alex sighed, pushing away from his desk and motioning for Victor to come over. "I don't know what's wrong with this thing."

"Let me see what you've done to her." Victor's sigh elicited a chuckle from his brother.

"*She* is right," Alex disgustedly agreed. "This thing is as temperamental as any woman I've ever known."

"You just don't know how to handle her," Victor chided as he continued typing on the keyboard, turning the screen completely black.

"I guess I don't," Alex agreed as he watched his brother work his magic. The man was a genius with computers.

Victor owned Delphine Computers and handled all the software needs for Alexander's. At twenty-nine, he was three years younger than Alex, and the two had always been close, especially since their parents died five years ago in a plane crash.

"There you go." Victor smiled with satisfaction a few minutes later. "She's as good as new."

Alex returned to his seat and tested out the computer. He heaved a sigh of relief when the blasted machine did what he wanted it to without fighting him.

"Thanks, man. You're a lifesaver."

"*De nada.*" Victor bowed before resuming his perch on the edge of Alex's desk. "By the way, who was the honey I saw leaving your office with Monique a few minutes ago?"

"That was our new junior associate, which means she's off-limits to you," Alex warned.

"She looked mad. What did you do to her?"

"I didn't do anything to her," Alex denied with a frown. "She took her sweet time about getting here, and I let her know I didn't appreciate it."

Victor's brows creased thoughtfully. "Is she the one from New York who had a last-minute funeral to attend?"

"A wedding," Alex corrected around a chuckle. "Her brother's, to be exact."

"Well, that was a good reason for the delay." Victor studied his brother's sour expression. "Wasn't it?"

"Yeah, I guess." Alex reclined in his chair.

"But?"

"If she was as dedicated as she *professes* to be, she would have been here on time."

"Come on Alex, it was her brother's wedding." He grinned. "You wouldn't miss my wedding, would you?"

"Definitely not." He twirled a pen in his fingers. "I'd be glad to be rid of you."

"You know you'd be bawling like a baby at the thought," Victor asserted.

"Yeah, go on and delude yourself." Alex laughed. "Anyway, we're not talking about me and what I would have done."

"Okay, point taken. What did she miss, really? Tell me." At his brother's silence, he admonished, "You need to lighten up, bro."

"I have a business to run, and I need dedicated people around me." Alex refused to give an inch.

"Who says she's not dedicated? She's here, isn't she?"

"Yeah." *She was here all right, upsetting his equilibrium.*

"Give the kid a break, Alex." Victor slapped him on the shoulder. "She's in a new country, starting a new job, and then she has to run into your foul temper." Victor sighed theatrically. "It's just too much for anyone to have to bear."

"Shouldn't you be somewhere doing something useful?" Alex chuckled in spite of himself.

"Not until this afternoon." Victor glanced without interest at his watch. "My morning's free."

"Well, I *do* have a lot of work to get through." Alex pointedly glanced at his brother before picking up some sketches from his desk to review.

Victor stood. "Oh, is that your not-so-subtle way of telling me to get lost?"

"We both know subtlety doesn't work with you." Alex grinned as his brother walked to the door.

"Just so you know, I don't appreciate being used and discarded," Victor huffed.

"You should be used to it by now," Alex good-naturedly rejoined.

"Sad, but true," Victor lamented. "Hey, tell you what."

"What?"

"I'll take the babe off your hands and escort her to the fashion show at the end of April," he magnanimously offered.

"No, I'll take her," Alex quickly asserted, having no idea why his brother's offer irritated him immensely.

"Ah-ha!" Victor shouted, and Alex grimaced. "So you *want* to take her then?"

"No, I don't want to take her," Alex quickly denied.

"Then let me," Victor offered again.

"It's my responsibility."

"You and your responsibility." Victor groaned in disgust.

"One of us has to be responsible," Alex drily asserted.

"You wound me, bro."

"You'll live," Alex promised. "Now will you get out of here?"

"Okay, I'm going. I think I'll see if I can spot…" He paused. "What's her name?"

"Nicole," Alex reluctantly offered. "Nicole Carter."

"Nicole…Nicole." Victor fit his tongue around her name with several different emphases. "Oh, I like that."

"Goodbye, Vic." Alex dismissed him, swiveling in his chair to stare moodily out of the window.

"See ya later, bro." Victor left, whistling a tune that grated on his brother's nerves.

Chapter 2

"Good morning, ladies." Victor entered the break room, pulled up a chair and sat down at Monique and Nicole's table. "Mind if I join you?"

Monique frowned at his actions. "Since you already have, that question is somewhat rhetorical, isn't it?"

"Oh, Monique." Victor chuckled and then turned his charm toward Nicole. "Hi, I'm Victor James."

"Nicole Carter." Nicole smiled when he brought her hand to his lips. "Nice to meet you, Mr. James."

"Please, I'm not that old. Mr. James was my father," Victor bemoaned. "Call me Victor or Vic."

"I will if you'll call me Nicole."

"Deal," he agreed. "Welcome to Alexander's."

"Thank you."

"And how are you today, beautiful?" He touched Monique's hand, which she quickly withdrew.

"I'm fine, Victor, and you?"

"Great now that I'm in the presence of two gorgeous ladies," he said. "What more could a guy want?"

"I'll pass on that one." Monique rolled her eyes and sipped her coffee.

"Coward," Victor softly teased before treating Nicole to another dazzling smile. "Whatever you've heard about me from Monique is untrue, unless you've been told I'm dashing, handsome and an all-around great guy."

"And modest," Monique sarcastically added, suppressing a smile when Victor stuck out his tongue at her.

"You can't be Alexander's brother." Nicole's stunned observation slipped from her lips before she could stop herself.

"I know." Victor shrugged. "What can I say? I have all of the charm."

Laughter bubbled from Nicole's lips. She was inclined to agree with him. He was easy to be around and didn't set her teeth on edge, and she immediately liked him.

"I didn't say that," Nicole reminded.

"No, I did, but don't tell Alex." His voice dropped to a whisper. "He's always been jealous because I'm the youngest and the better-looking one."

"And insecure, too," Monique drily added.

"Made so by your cruel barbs," Victor shot back, looking wounded.

"Just stating the facts as I see them."

Nicole studied Victor as he teased Monique. The James men were handsome. Victor was the same height and build as Alexander, and he had the same gorgeous eyes. However, his hair was cut very short, and his face sported a neatly trimmed goatee. They both possessed the same light skin tone, but Lord knew their personalities were as different as night and day.

"You two are certainly different in temperament," Nicole said.

"The poor guy just doesn't have my style." He shook his head sadly and sighed dramatically. "I worry about him so much."

Nicole chuckled, which turned into full-blown, tinkling laughter. Victor joined her, and even Monique was unsuccessful in suppressing a chuckle. Nicole felt as if she was among old friends. This day was turning out to be better than she had anticipated after her contentious first meeting with her straitlaced boss.

"I like you, Nicole," Victor confessed.

"I like you, too."

"You see." Victor grinned at Monique. "Nicole likes me."

"Give her time," Monique rejoined.

"Ouch!" Victor theatrically clutched at his heart. Nicole laughed, and a smile flirted about Monique's lips.

"Get out of here," Monique ordered. "We have business to discuss."

"In case you hadn't noticed, I'm part owner in Alexander's," Victor haughtily reminded her.

"Your brother runs the business. You're just the computer geek."

"I'd hardly think *owning* my own company qualifies me as a geek." Victor's faked outrage coerced a smile from Monique. "Besides, Alex runs Alexander's for two reasons. First, because it bears his name, and second, because he enjoys the tedious day-to-day operations, whereas I detest being chained to a desk."

"Yes, you do like to roam around, don't you?" Monique pointedly asked.

"Any and every chance I get." Merriment danced in Victor's eyes at Monique's loud sigh. "Now I'm leaving while I'm ahead," he proclaimed, grasping Nicole's hand and bringing it to his lips. "It was nice to meet you, Nicole. I'll be seeing you around." He winked at Monique and, before she could react, kissed her cheek and then left.

"Wow, he's certainly different from his brother," Nicole marveled.

"Thank goodness," Monique declared. "If Victor ran things, we'd never get any work done."

"I think he's nice and funny."

"Give the boss a chance. You'll like him once you get to know him."

Nicole's frown returned. "But will he like me?"

"Definitely," Monique promised. "Now, back to what we were talking about before Victor interrupted us. Are you going to take me up on my offer to move in with me?"

"It's nice of you to offer…"

"I'm not being nice," Monique interrupted, laughing. "I'm being selfish. My old roommate moved out a couple of months ago, and I've been searching for a new one, but I haven't liked any of the applicants. I know this is sudden, but I feel comfortable with you. I think we'd get along famously."

"Where is your apartment?" Nicole sipped her delicious coffee.

"In the 6th Arrondisement, close to your hotel. It's very spacious, six rooms, reasonable rent when shared and already furnished. However, you're free to change whatever you like," Monique continued to try to sell Nicole on the idea.

"It sounds wonderful."

"You can come by to look at it anytime you'd like," Monique offered. "And please take your time about deciding."

Nicole smiled as she considered Monique's offer. She had good instincts that seldom led her astray. She liked Monique, and it would be fun to stay with someone who knew Paris and could keep her from getting lonely being so far away from home.

"I'd love to be your new roommate," Nicole decided.

"Great!" Monique squeezed her hand. "I can help you move your stuff from the hotel. Just let me know when, and I'll be there."

"I'm afraid it'll have to wait until the weekend. I'm sure Mr. James will have me working late tonight and every night this week," Nicole direly predicted.

"He'll allow you some time off to move."

"No, I wouldn't dream of asking him." Nicole shook her head. "As much as I hate staying in a hotel—even one as beautiful as the Lutetia—it'll be my home for the rest of the week until my off day on Saturday. Okay?"

"Sure. I understand you want to put your best foot forward." Monique glanced at the clock. "To that end, we'd better get to work, or the boss will tear into both our hides."

"Please, I've had enough of that for one day." Nicole's groan and distasteful expression coaxed a chuckle from Monique.

"Come on then, I'll show you around the rest of the office," Monique offered, and they strolled out chatting as if they had been friends for years.

Nicole's rather spacious workstation was just outside of Monique's office. As Nicole glanced around the office, she felt it really was a designer's dream. A multitude of lights hung overhead, and windows lined nearly every wall, allowing plenty of natural light.

"The executive offices and designers are all housed on the sixth floor. The boss likes to keep us close," Monique informed. "What do you think of your new spot?"

"It's perfect. Much more than I expected." Nicole glanced around in awe. "I thought I'd be locked away in a cubbyhole."

"No way. I told you the boss takes care of us—especially

the designers." Monique laughed. "He told me he wanted you to start on the Bettina line."

"Yes." Nicole nodded. "He mentioned that to me, as well."

"Hang on a second." Monique disappeared into her office. Through the glass wall a few feet away, Nicole saw her rummage through papers on her desk until she found a white folder. She returned to Nicole and handed her the folder. "These are some notes, sketches and general info on the line, along with instructions on how to get into your PC where all of this info is located. Your temporary password is in here. You'll need to change it immediately."

"Thanks." Nicole flipped through the folder. "I can't wait to get started."

"I'll let you get to it. If you need anything, don't hesitate to ask." Monique squeezed her hand reassuringly. "I know you're going to do great, Nicole."

"Thanks, Monique."

Preparing to get settled, Nicole took out pictures of family and placed them on her desk, lovingly fingering one of the silver frames, then opened her portfolio and started setting up her workstation the way she wanted it. Finally, she opened her sketch book, switched on her PC, spread out notes on the Bettina line across her desk and prepared to start work on her first design for Alexander's. She was determined it was going to knock Alexander James's socks off.

Two hours later, a little before ten, Monique stopped by her station and tapped her on the shoulder.

"I forgot to tell you, the boss likes to have staff meetings every Monday at ten. I'll show you how to set up your calendar when we get back."

"Okay." Nicole stood and picked up a notebook and pen.

"Use this for notes. It's easier." Monique handed her

a tablet. "This one is yours. It has our design software on it—the same that's on your laptop. Feel free to take it home. I take mine everywhere."

"Thanks." Nicole eyed her expensive tablet. "Mr. James doesn't skimp, does he?"

"I told you the boss is good to us," Monique reminded her. "Let's get going. He hates it when people are late."

"Uh yes, I've noticed that about him." Nicole's fervent whisper provoked a sympathetic smile from Monique as they walked toward the conference room.

Thankfully, they were the first to arrive at the meeting, save Alexander James, who sat at the head of an enormous oval oak table. He had removed his jacket and had rolled up his shirtsleeves, revealing hair-covered, sinewy forearms. He nodded at them when they entered and then returned his attention to his computer. Nicole and Monique chatted quietly as other staff filed in. Nicole felt the hair on the back of her neck standing up and turned to find a blond woman staring at her with blatant hostility. Where was that coming from?

"Hey," Nicole whispered in Monique's ear. "Who is that woman?"

Monique glanced in the direction Nicole covertly pointed with a tilt of her head. "Oh, that's Crystal Danforth. Don't pay any attention to her."

"Did I do something to her?"

"No, Crystal doesn't much like anyone, but she is an excellent designer," Monique grudgingly admitted, "which is why the boss keeps her around."

"Oh." Nicole glanced up and met Alexander's intense gaze briefly before he busied himself with his computer again.

"Don't sweat it." Monique winked and added, "If she gives you any trouble, she'll answer to me, and I outrank her."

Nicole smiled at Monique's threat and glanced at Crystal again, who treated her to another hateful stare before focusing her eyes on her tablet.

So much for not having any enemies in the office. Nicole silently sighed.

Within ten minutes, the room was full. After everyone was settled in with coffee, juice and pastries, Alexander began the meeting.

"You all know Victor." Alex pointed to his brother, who was sitting to his right. "For some reason, he insists on loitering around the office today."

Victor smiled. "You know you miss me when I'm not here."

"Yeah, right." Alexander chuckled. "Why are you here today anyway?"

"Three reasons." Victor stood. "First, I had to fix your computer for you after you mistreated her," he reminded his brother with a wink, which caused chuckles from around the room. "Second, I'm doing an upgrade on everyone's computer." He laughed at the groans and surveyed the twenty people in the room. "Hey, do you guys want to be state of the art or what? I promise the downtime won't be long."

"Promises, promises," Monique drawled, drawing Victor's interest.

"I always keep my promises," Victor softly responded.

"Hmph!" Monique didn't sound convinced.

"And three?" Alexander queried, interrupting their banter.

"I don't have anything better to do." Victor sighed and resumed his seat amid laughter.

"That's my brother, folks." Alexander shook his head in mock disgust.

"You know you love me," Victor taunted.

"Be quiet," Alex admonished and chuckled when Victor made a zipping motion across his lips. "All right, down to business. As you all know, we have a new associate designer, Nicole Carter, who comes to us all the way from New York—albeit a little late."

Nicole's smile faded slightly as he added the latter, and she bit her lower lip to hold in the angry retort that was trying desperately to escape from her mouth. She purposefully brightened her smile in response to the various welcomes from her coworkers before resuming eye contact with Alexander.

"I know you'll all make her feel welcome. She'll be working on the Bettina line, and I'm counting on those of you who are also assigned there to quickly get her up to speed."

"She'll be there in no time, boss," Monique chimed in, and Nicole shot her a grateful smile.

"With your help, I'm sure she will." Alexander nodded with a slight smile. "We have our early-spring fashion show at the end of April, so I'm expecting a hundred and ten percent from everyone." Nicole bristled again when his eyes rested on her. "We'll probably be going to a six-day workweek in a week or so."

Victor glanced at Nicole and mouthed, "Don't mind him."

Nicole sighed visibly and Victor chuckled.

Alex caught Nicole and Victor's subtle exchange, and his eyes narrowed on his brother's seemingly innocent face just in time to see him wink at Nicole, who, much to his annoyance, returned his gesture. Why the friendly interaction between the two irritated him to no end he was loath to examine.

"Do you mind?" Alex frowned at his brother. "I'm trying to run a meeting here."

"Be my guest, bro." Victor leaned back in his seat, crossed his arms and waited for Alex to continue.

"Thank you," Alex sarcastically said. "If you'd all turn your attention to your tablets and pull up the memo I sent this morning, I'd like to start with that."

As Alex presided over the meeting, he found it next to impossible to keep his eyes from straying toward Nicole more often than not, which annoyed him to no end. She sat there with a frown on her beautiful face, unless she was smiling at Monique—or Victor, which peeved him. He knew she was shooting daggers at him because of his earlier reference to her delayed start with the company, and although he shouldn't care, he did.

Alex glanced away from his presentation to answer a question, and his eyes automatically stopped to stare at Nicole—even though she wasn't the one asking the question. She held his gaze for a second before tilting her head in Monique's direction, who was whispering something in her ear that made her smile. She was gorgeous when she smiled.

Oh, hell!

Somehow he concentrated on answering the question at hand, but he was acutely aware of his newest employee—he noticed everything she did, when she smiled, said something to Monique, crossed her legs, sighed. With her mere presence, she was disrupting his neatly ordered world, and he didn't like it!

Thankfully, the rest of the meeting was spent discussing designs, fabrics and the order for the upcoming fashion show. The hour breezed by.

"Good work, everyone. That'll be all." Alexander adjourned the meeting, and the room quickly emptied. "Nicole, could you stay behind please?"

She glanced at Monique, who patted her reassuringly on the back as she resumed her seat, crossed her legs and folded her hands in her lap. Victor gave her an encouraging thumbs-up sign, to which she smiled. Both she and Alex waited until the room was empty before speaking.

"Did Monique show you the Bettina line info?"

"Yes."

"Do you have any questions?"

"Not presently." She kept her responses brief and crisp.

He frowned. "Is anything wrong?"

"No, nothing." She shrugged and pursed her lips, but the words continued to flow. "I so enjoy being embarrassed in front of my new colleagues." His lips thinned at her flippant tone.

"I didn't mean to embarrass you."

"Didn't you?"

"No, I was simply stating the facts," he coolly replied. "If your skin is this thin, you're never going to make it around here."

She stiffened her back at his rebuke. "My skin is plenty thick enough, Mr. James."

"We'll see," he darkly promised.

"Yes, you will." She uncrossed her legs. "Is there anything else?"

He stared at her long and hard, and she didn't flinch or look away. "No, that's all for now."

She stood and left without another word. Alone, he smiled slightly. She was a spitfire. He'd soon see what she was made of, and he had a feeling he would enjoy doing it.

The days flew by, and before Nicole knew it, the week was half-over. On Wednesday evening, she absently returned numerous goodbyes from her coworkers, including Monique, and continued happily working. She barely registered that bright sunlight had given way to pale moonlight. When she glanced at the clock, it was after 8:30 p.m.

She studied her sketch and smiled. Picking up her charcoal pencil, she continued working on the lines of the skirt she was sketching. Just a few more minutes, and she would call it a day.

"It's way past quitting time." Nicole jumped, then glanced up when Alexander's voice disturbed the comforting silence.

"Mr. James." She placed a hand against her thudding heart. "You scared the life out of me."

"Sorry." He pulled up a tall stool and sat beside her.

"I thought everyone had gone home." She was acutely aware of his closeness.

"Everyone has, except us." He glanced at her sketch, picked it up and then replaced it on the easel. His face was unreadable.

"What do you think of it?" She asked simply to have something to say.

"It's adequate." He half smiled at her apparent displeasure with his blasé description.

"Adequate?" She glanced at the drawing she had spent the entire day revising, intent that it would be perfect before she showed it to him. "What's wrong with it?"

"Nothing's wrong with it," he insisted. "It's not finished, is it?"

"No."

"Then I think adequate is an appropriate assessment," he rationalized. "I need to see the finished product before I know whether it fits with the Bettina line."

"Of course."

He cocked his head to one side. "That displeases you?"

"No." She drew out the single syllable. "You're right, of course."

"I know I'm right."

They stared at each other silently. She contemplated what to say next. She didn't want to be constantly at odds with him. She wanted them to get along and have a good

working relationship; therefore, she bit back the angry retort that was on the verge of jumping from her mouth.
When she spoke next, her voice was calm and measured.

"I really want this job to go well," she softly admitted. "I know I was late. I've apologized, but I couldn't
miss my brother's wedding. My love for my family doesn't
mean I'm not dedicated to being the best designer I can
be. I know I can learn a lot from you—if you'll give me a
chance. That's all I'm asking, Mr. James."

He silently studied her long and hard. He had expected
an angry rejoinder to his frankly baiting previous statement; she had surprised him again. Her sincere plea affected him more than anything else she could have said.

"You're talented, Nicole. You wouldn't have gotten the
job otherwise." He paused before admitting, "I'm not sorry
I hired you." Her eyes brightened at his admission, and he
was absurdly glad.

"You're not?"

"No." He smiled slightly. "I think you have great po-
tential, and from what I've seen of your work so far, if
you apply yourself, you'll make a name for yourself in
this business."

"Well…" She seemed at a loss for words at his gener-
ous compliment.

"Nothing to say?" he teased.

"I… Thank you."

"You're welcome." He suddenly stood. "Now close up
shop and go home."

"But I wanted to finish…"

"No buts." He switched off her light, took her hands
and pulled her to her feet. "Go home."

"All right."

He released her hands, picked up her jacket and held it
out for her. As she slipped it on, he felt her nearness. His

hands rested on her upper arms for a second longer than necessary. She slowly turned around and looked at him, and he swore he saw desire in her eyes, but it was gone so quickly, he wasn't sure—although he definitely felt the heat between them.

"Can I give you a lift to the hotel?" *Why had he said that?*

"No." She took a few steps away from him. "I'll take the metro."

"You're in a new city. I don't like the thought of you taking the metro by yourself at night."

"I'll be fine," she assured. "I'm a big girl, Mr. James."

"Yes, I've noticed." He couldn't keep from sweeping his eyes appreciatively over her from head to toe and back again. "Mr. James was my dad. Call me Alex." He frowned when she smiled and laughed lightly. "What?"

"Victor said exactly the same thing when I called him Mr. James," she explained.

"Oh, I see." He nodded in understanding but felt a twinge of something he was loath to name at the mention of his brother and her sharing a private moment. "Come on, let's call it a night."

She hesitated for a second and then gave in and preceded him out.

Chapter 3

Once the elevator doors closed, for the first time in her life, Nicole experienced claustrophobia—the result of being alone in a confined space with Alexander. This man was too enigmatic for his own good—and, more important, for hers. What in reality was a quick ride down to the lobby seemed to take forever. When finally the doors opened, Nicole breathed a silent sigh of relief, though she expected her relief would be short-lived once she was trapped with Alexander in the close confines of what she instinctively knew would be a tiny sports car.

They said good-night to the guard and walked out. When they reached the curb, confirming her silent suspicions, a flame-red Ferrari convertible was waiting for them.

"Thanks for bringing my car around, Jacques." Alexander patted the guard on the back.

"No problem, Mr. James." Jacques smiled. "I enjoy any chance to drive such a fine machine."

"She's something, isn't she?" Alex proudly glanced at his car.

"And then some," Jacques agreed before walking back into the building.

"Wow." Nicole's eyes widened appreciatively as they traveled over the sleek curvaceous lines of the car that reminded her of the man about to drive it—sleek, powerful and gorgeous. Alexander opened the door and helped her inside before walking around and sliding behind the wheel.

The rich smell of leather assailed her. The black-and-tan dashboard and steering wheel contained a multitude of controls. It looked like a complicated airplane panel. For a car that cost upward of $300,000, she would expect nothing less.

"How do you like my baby?" He caressed the black leather steering wheel, and his left thumb pressed a button to start the car. The powerful engine roared to life, and he wasn't even depressing the accelerator. "She'll go from zero to sixty in three seconds."

"She's stunning." Nicole sighed gratefully as the contoured tan leather seat conformed to her body as if custom made for her. "Breathtaking."

Alex flashed a quick grin. "Fast cars are one of my vices."

"One?" She cocked a teasing eyebrow. "How many vices do you have?"

"A few." His grin transformed into a devilish smile. "Fasten your seat belt." Once she did, he sped off. When he noticed her right hand clutching the armrest he asked, "You're not afraid of a little speed are you?"

"Not at all," Nicole said. "It's just that the engine is so loud and menacing."

"Oh, it is. This baby can really eat up the road."

"You can say that again." Nicole tensed as his *baby* proved his point.

"Relax." Alex reassuringly squeezed her left knee. "I promise to get you to the hotel safely."

Suddenly her apprehension at being a passenger in such a powerful machine vanished. Alexander's touch ignited forbidden passions within her. Even through the material of her pants, where his hand rested, her skin burned. Her eyes pivoted from his hand resting comfortably on her knee back to his profile.

As if realizing what he had unconsciously done, he removed his hand quickly and placed it on the center console. Neither of them made mention of his actions, but each was keenly aware of them.

For the remainder of the drive, they said little and the tension between them grew as thick as dense fog. The spicy smell of his aftershave was driving her mad until she wanted to bury her nose in the crook of his neck and inhale deeply. What a handsome man. *Stop that, Nicole,* she silently ordered. *He's your boss.*

The drive was short due to the speed at which he drove, His speed thankfully was somewhat constrained by traffic. She occasionally glanced at him, but his eyes remained focused on the road ahead.

He came to a screeching stop in front of her hotel not a second too soon to save Nicole's sanity. The doorman opened her door before Alexander could, but Alexander was there to take her hand and help her out of the car.

"Well, here we are," he announced.

"And in one piece." She placed a hand to her heart, and he chuckled.

"Come on, my driving's not that bad, is it?"

"No. This is an insanely powerful car, but you handle her beautifully."

He liked the way she referred to his car as a person the way he did. Most women simply rolled their eyes when men personalized inanimate objects, but not Nicole. That was a mark in her favor—not that he was counting.

"Thanks." He followed her into the lobby, still holding her hand easily. "Once you drive one of these babies, you'll never be satisfied with anything else."

"Well, that's not likely to happen."

"Never say never," he softly chided and then easily offered, "One day I'll teach you to drive her."

"I'd be too terrified to attempt it," Nicole declined with a smile.

"She'll be putty in your hands."

"Or I'll be putty in hers."

"Don't worry. I have a feeling you can handle her just fine."

His fingers absently caressed hers, and he heard her soft gasp at his subconscious actions. She pulled her hand from his, and he was keenly aware of the increased tempo in the pulse beating at the base of her neck. He longed to caress the spot with his lips and tongue. *What was he thinking?* Suddenly, nothing seemed more important than that he stay and spend some time alone with her, getting to know her better. But that overwhelming desire was one he dared not succumb to.

She's your employee, Alex. You're not going down that road again! You know what happened the last time.

"Good night." He abruptly turned to leave. "See you in the morning."

"Bright and early," she promised. "Thanks for the ride."

"You're welcome." He walked away before he succumbed to the overwhelming need to stay.

Nicole slowly walked to the elevator and entered. When she glanced up, Alexander was standing near the doorway, watching her. Her breath arrested at the look in his eyes— a look needing no definition or interpretation with words.

Thankfully the doors closed, shutting him out of her view but not out of her mind.

"He's your boss, Nicole," she forcefully reminded herself again. "That's all he'll ever be."

Yes, that's what she repeatedly told herself, but she couldn't beat back the nagging voice and feeling inside of her that challenged that assertion. Why, oh, why did she have to have these inappropriate feelings for Alexander?

Oh, Lord, she was in big trouble, and she had no earthly idea of how she was going to get out of it.

Bright and early the next morning, after a somewhat restless night spent thinking about her worrisome attraction to Alexander, Nicole arrived at work at 7:00 a.m., and by 8:00, she had already downed five cups of coffee. Her excessive beverage intake necessitated a few trips to the ladies' room. On her way back to her desk, she passed by Alexander's slightly ajar door and quickly recognized Alexander and Victor's voices.

She had every intention of walking on by, but her feet became glued to the spot when her name was mentioned. She knew she shouldn't eavesdrop, but curiosity to hear what they were saying about her kept her rooted in place. Unfortunately, when she heard Alex question her commitment after he had told her last night he didn't regret hiring her, any semblance of common sense flew straight out the window.

Without thinking, Nicole pushed open Alexander's door the rest of the way and walked inside, glancing from one startled brother to the other. Her defiant eyes immediately landed on Alexander's displeased ones.

"When gossiping about someone," she sweetly began, "it's prudent to make certain your door is closed to minimize the risk of being overheard."

"Yes." Alex folded his muscular arms over his broad chest. "It's also wise to account for snoops."

"I wasn't snooping." At Alexander's skeptical stare she continued, "I was simply passing by and heard my name. Naturally, I was curious."

"Naturally," Alex sarcastically agreed.

"Nicole, I apologize…" Victor began.

"Don't worry about it, Victor." Nicole gave him a slight smile before returning angry eyes to his brother.

"So it's safe to assume your anger is reserved for me alone." Alex bristled. It exasperated him to no end that she didn't seem the least bit miffed at Victor, who had also been discussing her. "Is that right?"

"You know what they say about assuming, don't you?" Nicole softly asked, her anger dissipating instantaneously.

"You know what they say about curiosity and the cat, don't you?" Alex shot back without answering her question.

"Yes, I do," she pleasantly assured him. "But do you know that after curiosity killed the cat, satisfaction brought it back?"

Victor chuckled, Alex snarled and Nicole smiled triumphantly at getting the last word before leaving them alone and closing the door behind her with a decisive click.

"Damn, she's something," Victor approved, and Alex silently agreed. "That'll teach you to complain about your employees publicly."

"Yeah, I was complaining all to myself, wasn't I?" Alex frowned at Victor.

"I was merely being a sounding board so you wouldn't take your foul mood out on your staff," Victor informed.

"You're such a humanitarian," Alex sarcastically rejoined.

"What can I say?" Victor shrugged. "I do what I can."

"Get out of here, Vic." Alex sighed, reclining against his desk. "You've caused me enough trouble for one day."

"Me? Trouble?" Victor pointed to himself. "Surely you jest."

"No, I don't," Alex said. "You're nothing but bad news."

"My dear brother, you know your life would be so boring without me."

"Oh, how I'd like to test that theory." Despite his black mood, Alex cracked a smile.

"No, you wouldn't." Victor confidently grinned and opened the door. "Later, bro."

"Hey." Alex halted his brother's exit. "What do they say about assuming?"

"You're kidding, right?" At his brother's blank stare, Victor laughed heartily before explaining, "When you assume you make an *ass* out of *u* and *me*. Get it?"

"Ah, I see." Alex smirked at his brother, who gave him a mock salute before exiting. Well, she had told him off without raising that sweet little sexy voice of hers, hadn't she?

He glanced at his closed door, and his smirk transformed into a slight smile as he replayed the confrontation with Nicole. Today she was dressed in a red dress with a matching duster jacket and red pumps. She looked wonderful and smelled even better—like lavender. He had fought down an insane urge to bury his nose in her neck and inhale deeply. *What the...?* His smile quickly slid into a deep frown. *Oh, Lord, what am I doing reminiscing over how she looked and smelled?*

She had barged into his office uninvited, so he should be angry; however, he was intrigued instead—which was surprising and intensely disquieting. Nicole Carter had that effect on him. The question was, what was he going to do about it?

* * *

As Nicole slowly made her way to her workstation, she chewed on her lower lip worriedly. What in the world had possessed her to do such a stupid thing like confronting her boss like that? Even though his door had been ajar, he had been in the privacy of his office talking to his brother, and she should have just walked on by.

She wasn't impulsive, and now was no time to change her ways; she usually weighed everything she said and did very carefully. *You're sleep deprived. That's why you acted so unwisely,* she told herself to feel better, but it wasn't working. She sat down at her desk and sighed heavily.

She was used to order and normalcy in her life. Since moving to Paris, her equilibrium had been constantly in flux—due primarily to her volatile boss and her disturbing attraction to him. She didn't know where she stood with Alexander from one second to the next. She had thought after last night that they were starting to get along, but after overhearing him complaining about her this morning, she wasn't sure anymore.

She wanted Alexander's respect and maybe even his admiration. They had gotten off on the wrong foot, and the little scene she had just caused probably hadn't helped things. She half expected him to barge out of his office, tell her off in front of everyone and order her out of his company, but thankfully, he didn't. Apparently she was still employed at her dream job—for the time being anyway.

Resting her chin on her hands, she silently reprimanded her unruly tongue, which had caused her far too much trouble so early in the morning.

The next time Nicole saw Alexander was in the late morning. He was walking around the designers' workstations peering over shoulders, making suggestions and giving out compliments when he deemed warranted. After their confrontation this morning, she held her breath, praying he would bypass her. Of course, he didn't.

He reached her station and sat down beside her. She had removed her jacket, leaving her arms bare. When he slid his chair close to hers, the sleeve of his jacket brushed against her bare flesh, sending tremors through her.

"Settling in?"

"Yes." She managed a slight smile. "Monique is great."

"She is," he agreed. "You seem startled. Why?"

"You know why," she softly accused.

"You're right. I do." He paused before adding, "I apologize for talking about you behind your back. I shouldn't have done that."

Her eyes widened. "You're apologizing to me?"

"Yes, I am. Do you accept my apology?"

He had completely flabbergasted her. Where was the anger and outrage she expected from him? This man was truly hard to figure out; she never knew what he was going to say or do next.

"Of course I do. Thank you." She magnanimously added, "I'm sorry for barging into your office."

"It's already forgotten." He waved her apology away. "You may have figured out that I can be very demanding, Nicole."

"Yes, I had noticed that," Nicole quickly agreed around a smile.

"Right." Humor lit up his gorgeous eyes. "I'm going to be hard on you, but I promise to give you a fair shot."

"I can't ask for anything more than that."

"Truce?" He offered his hand.

"Truce." She placed her hand in his momentarily, but that was long enough for needles of awareness to shoot through her. "I'm looking forward to working here, Alexander."

"And work you will," he assured before standing and leaving her staring after him.

Seconds later, Monique walked out of her office to perch on the edge of Nicole's desk. "Hey, girl."

"Hey." Nicole tore her attention from Alexander's retreating back and focused on her colleague.

"You and the boss looked rather cozy."

"He was just showing me something."

"Really?" Monique grinned. "Do tell, what?"

"Something about work," Nicole said with a shake of her head.

"Oh, okay." Nicole raised an eyebrow at her skeptical tone. "You're starting to like him, aren't you?"

"He's—" Nicole paused, unsure of how to finish that sentence. Finally, she ended, "—very complicated."

"Truly," Monique agreed.

"I never know what he's going to do or say." Nicole glanced around to make sure he wasn't within earshot. "He's so…temperamental."

"He definitely is. I think it's the artist in him. He's also very fair."

"I hope so."

"Trust me, he is." Monique couldn't resist adding, "You'll find that out soon enough."

"Here's the sketch you asked me to revise."

"Nice subject change." Monique took the sketch from her and studied it. "Very good. I like it a lot."

"I'm glad."

"You've got talent, girl. I see why the boss hired you."

Nicole placed a hand on her hip in fake outrage. "Did you ever doubt it?"

"Never." Monique smiled. "Work me up two variations of this sketch—one with a longer skirt and the other with a different top."

"I'm on it." Nicole flipped to a clean page in her draft book. "When do you need them?"

"How does tomorrow around noon sound?"

"Perfect."

"Great. I'll let you get back to work." Monique stood. "If you have any questions, holler."

"Will do," Nicole agreed, reaching for her charcoal pencil and bending her head to study the sketch on her desk.

Her hand froze in midair as the hair on the back of her neck stood on end. She felt rather than saw Alexander's eyes on her. Slowly glancing up, she found him standing across the room at Crystal's desk. He was nodding as though listening to something she was saying, but his eyes were glued on Nicole. She returned his intense stare for a few seconds before lowering her eyes back to her sketch, pretending interest in her design when she was really wondering what that look was all about.

Chapter 4

Around noon, Nicole had finished one of Monique's requested revisions of her sketch and was starting on the second when the hair on the back of her neck stood up in rapt attention. Instinctively, she knew Alexander had entered the designers' area. It was uncanny that she could *feel* him before she saw him.

He stopped to answer a question from another designer. Nicole heard him laugh heartily, which was a sound she could really get used to. She held her breath involuntarily, praying he wouldn't stop by her station, which, of course, he did.

He stood beside her desk silently for a few seconds, willing her to look at him. She knew she couldn't ignore him and slowly raised her eyes to his.

"You're not using Victor's design software?"

"I've played with it, and it's fabulous," Nicole carefully began.

"But?" Alex smiled slightly. At her hesitation he ordered, "Be perfectly honest."

"But when I first create a design, I have to do it with my charcoal pencil and paper." She shrugged. "It allows me to *feel* the design. I don't know how else to explain it."

"You explained it perfectly," Alex assured. "I know exactly what you mean."

Nicole sighed in relief that she hadn't offended him. "You, too?"

"Yep."

"I'm glad I'm not the only weird one."

"Hardly." Alex winked, pulled up a chair beside her and sat down. "May I steal of piece of your paper?"

"Of course." Nicole tore off a couple of sheets from her pad and handed them to him, along with a charcoal pencil.

"I'm going to start a design." He began effortlessly sketching. "And you're going to finish it."

Nicole's heart jumped into her throat at his casual, terrifying statement. Was he serious? The walls started closing in on her, and she gulped in air. She glanced down at his hands as they expertly glided over the paper, and the formations of an elegant beaded blouse began to take shape. *Oh, Lord, please let me remember how to sketch,* she silently prayed.

"Okay." He handed her the paper and charcoal. "Your turn."

Nicole cautiously took the pencil from him and held it between her shaking fingers. She willed her nerves to subside; however, they persisted mercilessly.

"I'm not sure what you want." Nicole's terrified eyes stared into his serious ones.

"I want you to revise my design any way you see fit to make it better," he elaborated.

"You want me to make *your* design better?"

He chuckled at her incredulity. "Yes."

"Okay," she nervously agreed. "I'll try."

How was she supposed to improve on Alexander James's design? She swallowed her apprehension, took a calming breath and started revising as requested. After hesitating endlessly, she finally added jeweled cuffs to the sheer sleeves to match the neckline, which she changed from the square design Alexander had created into a sweetheart one. Last, she lengthened the blouse by an inch.

When she finished he didn't say a word, simply took the charcoal from her and sketched a pencil skirt, followed by a ball gown. He handed the sketches and charcoal back to her, which she took and immediately began revising. The only design he rerevised was the ball gown and insisted she do the same. They spent about forty minutes together designing, and it was nerve-racking, but also exhilarating.

"How did I do?" She held her breath.

For a few minutes Alex studied the three designs they had created without responding. She fought against tapping her fingers impatiently on the desktop or shaking him to get an answer; instead, she folded her hands in her lap and waited for his critique.

"Very nice," he finally answered, and she frowned.

"Is that good?"

"That's good." At his assurance, she released her heretofore held breath on an audible sigh. "Well done."

"That was nerve-racking," she admitted with a slight smile.

"I know." He touched her hand briefly. "Come on, wasn't it just a little bit fun?"

"It was—now that it's over." She laughed, and he joined her.

"Which is your favorite?" He spread the designs out on her desk for her review.

"The ball gown."

"Mine, too."

He picked up the design and studied it. Their codesign was floor length, free-flowing and simply elegant. It was Grecian-inspired, sleeveless, cut into a deep V nearly to the waist, which was gathered with a wide sequined belt, and the skirt cascaded down to the floor in soft folds.

"What material would you use for this?"

"Chiffon." Nicole decided without hesitation. "This gown was made for layers and layers of chiffon."

"I agree," Alex said approvingly. "I think this might have a place in our April fashion show."

Nicole's eyes dilated to twice their normal size. Surely he was teasing her. Wasn't he?

"Are you serious?"

"Absolutely." Alex smiled at her shocked expression. "This will be the first James-Carter creation."

Nicole was too flabbergasted and thrilled to respond to this fantastic news. She didn't know which was more thrilling—designing a gown with him or the fact that he had referred to it as their *first* one. Somebody pinch her; she was going to codesign a gown for a fashion show with Alexander James!

"Wow." She wasn't aware of speaking out loud, but Alexander's chuckle informed her she had.

"I hear Monique asked you to move in with her."

"What?" Nicole blinked rapidly at his change in subject.

"I said I heard that Monique asked you to move in with her."

"Oh. Yes, she did."

"She told me you refused to relocate until the weekend because of work," he continued.

Nicole groaned. "I wish she hadn't said anything to you."

"Why?"

"Because…" She faltered, unwilling to finish verbalizing her reasons.

"You thought I'd make a big deal if you asked to take the time off to move," he correctly completed for her.

"It's not a problem," she quickly guaranteed. "I'm fine with moving over the weekend, Mr. James."

"Alex," he reminded with a smile.

"Alexander." She opted for the full version instead. "I don't expect nor do I want any special privileges."

"And you won't get any," he quickly assured. "Nicole, you've relocated from another country. You're entitled to time off to move. Leave here at two today, and get yourself situated at your new place."

"But…"

"That's an order," he commanded in mock sternness. "Just make sure you're here bright and early in the morning."

"I will be," she promised as he stood. "Thank you, Mr.—I mean, Alexander."

"You're welcome."

He studied the designs she had been working on before he interrupted her. "That's nice. You're working on a variation of this?"

"Two. Monique wanted one with a different top and another with a longer skirt."

"Why don't you also do one that shortens the hem by half an inch and add a slight flare to the skirt?"

"I will."

"What type of material are you thinking of using?"

"It's meant for casual wear, so I was entertaining jersey knit for freedom of movement and ease of care."

"Good choice." His eyes strayed to her desk to the pictures arranged there. "Your family?"

She followed his eyes and smiled. "Yes."

"May I?" He pointed toward the wedding photo showing them all.

"Please." She handed him the photo.

"Your brother's wedding?"

"Yes." She waited for a snide remark, and when none came, she relaxed and pointed everyone out. "That's Nathan and Marcy. That's my sister Natasha and her husband, Damien—who's Marcy's brother." She paused and glanced at him. "Are you following me?"

"Yeah, I think so." He chuckled. "There wasn't a brother free for you?"

"Nope, the Johnsons were fresh out of siblings."

"Are you sad about that?"

"No, I don't need to be fixed up. I'll find my own man when I'm ready." How had the conversation taken such a personal turn? It was too weird and very uncomfortable talking to her boss about finding a man to settle down with.

"So you're not ready now?"

"No, I'm focused on establishing my career."

"That's commendable."

She purposefully refocused his attention to the photo and concluded. "That's my mother, father and Marcy and Damien's parents."

"And you."

She smiled. "And me."

"You have a nice-looking family."

"Thank you." She took the photo from him and replaced it on her desk. "I love them."

"It shows when you talk about them." As if sensing she was missing them, he changed the subject. "The wedding dress is beautiful. Who designed it?"

"I did," she proudly proclaimed.

"You?" At her nod, he picked up the picture again. "It's really lovely."

"Thank you.

"What about the bridesmaids' dresses?"

"Me again. I even made them."

He whistled in admiration at her statement, and she felt ten feet tall.

"You sew, too?"

"Since I was nine."

"That's damned good work, Nicole."

"Thank you again." This was turning out to be a fabulous day. "I'm not used to so many compliments from you."

"Get used to them," he suggested.

He stood and walked away without another word, and Nicole shook her head in confusion. That man was a whirlwind of unpredictability.

He had certainly changed her opinion of him in record time. It seemed he could be both human and appealing when he wanted to. But she wasn't sure which Alexander she preferred—the gruff one who set her teeth on the edge, or the likable one who she longed to get to know better—and not in a professional way.

Nicole left work at two and changed into faded jeans, a red "I Love NY" T-shirt, a denim jacket and sneakers. Monique had gone home to change and was meeting her at the hotel at three. Thankfully, the move wouldn't involve any furniture, just clothes, though Nicole had a lot.

She hadn't unpacked most of her bags, for which she was grateful. She stood in the middle of the sitting room, where she had gathered almost everything, and groaned at the rather large pile in front of her. A few bags were still in her hotel bedroom. Goodness, had she really packed this much stuff?

She was shaking her head in self-recrimination when someone knocked on her door. Expecting Monique, she opened the door and gasped in shock when she found Alexander and Victor dressed casually in jeans, T-shirts and light jackets.

"What are you two doing here?"

"We've come to make amends for our faux pas earlier." Victor glanced at the pile of her belongings inside the room. "Looks like you can use our help."

"You don't have to help me move." Nicole directed her words to the silent Alexander. "I'm sure you have better things to do with your day."

"We want to." Alexander finally spoke. "May we come in?"

"I'm sorry." Nicole stepped aside to allow them in. "Come in."

"Is this all that's going?" Victor pointed to the stack of luggage piled on and beside the sofa.

"Most of it. There's some more in my bedroom."

"I'll start on these. Alex, why don't you see what's in the bedroom?"

"All right." Alex glanced at Nicole, who pointed the way and then quickly followed him, praying she didn't have any unmentionables lying about. Thankfully, the coast was clear.

"I can manage this," Alexander assured her after surveying the small stack of bags. "Why don't you go and help Victor?"

"Are you sure? I can take…oh!"

She stumbled over a suitcase on the floor and wound up flying toward Alexander. He caught her effortlessly, strong arms automatically encircling her off-balance body. He held her tight against his unyielding strength.

All air left Nicole's lungs, more from the close proximity to Alexander than from the impact of landing against his hard chest. Both appeared frozen in their unplanned yet potent embrace. Her palms rested flat against his broad chest cushioned by solid muscles. His hands rested on her waist. Their eyes locked, and each was aware that their mouths were only inches apart. A fact that became crystal clear when Alexander's eyes darted to her slightly parted lips and stayed focused there as if mesmerized.

She held her breath while she waited to see what would happen next. She didn't have to wait long. Unable to help himself, Alex lowered his mouth to hers. Their lips touched lightly several times before they both sought out much longer contact, and when they achieved it, time froze.

Their lips flirted, pressed lightly, pulled away. Alex's teeth nibbled softly at her lower lip before sending his tongue to investigate the same territory. Nicole shuddered. Her arms snaked up his chest to rest into his hard shoulders as she moved and was pulled closer to his unbending length. She sighed and parted her lips invitingly, and her eyes fluttered close in anticipation of a deeper, more satisfying kiss.

"Nicole!" Victor shouted, splintering the intimate moment. "Monique is here."

"I...I'll be right out," Nicole breathlessly replied, moving guiltily out of Alexander's arms, placing fingers to her tingling lips. "Excuse me."

"Of course." Alex managed a slight smile as she skirted around him and out the bedroom door.

Oh, Lord, what had she done? She let out her breath on a noisy sigh. The chaste kisses they had shared didn't begin to quench her disturbing desire for her boss, only managed to inflame it further. She didn't know whether to be relieved or disappointed with Victor's interruption, but she was certainly unfulfilled.

"Hi, roomie," Monique greeted Nicole as she entered the room. "I see we have help."

"Yes." Nicole prayed she didn't look as flustered as she felt. "Alexander is here, too. He's in the bedroom."

Monique grinned. "Is that where you're coming from?"

"Yes." Nicole pushed her bangs out of her eyes with somewhat shaky fingers.

"Why do you look so flushed?" Monique's knowing grin caused Nicole to shift uncomfortably. "What was going on in there?"

"I… We…" Nicole floundered but thankfully Alexander entered, arms laden with luggage, and ushered Victor out the door. Nicole envied his composure.

"Hi, Monique." Alex nodded as he passed by her.

"Hi, boss," Monique greeted before refocusing on Nicole. "Is your lipstick smudged?"

"I…um…" Nicole absently touched her lips. "Must have happened as I packed."

"Mmm-hmm." Monique's wide grin informed Nicole she wasn't buying her lame explanation.

To avoid any further inquisition, Nicole grabbed a bag and hurried after the two men. Monique laughed, picked up a suitcase herself and followed her fellow movers out.

When they reached her new home a short while later, Nicole was pleased to realize Monique hadn't exaggerated; the apartment was lovely and spacious. It was located in a picturesque part of the 6th Arrondisement and had shining hardwood floors and a myriad of windows and was decorated in brightly colored, comfortable furniture with lots of cushions. Nicole's bedroom and bathroom was next to Monique's. The living area was huge, and the kitchen was perfect. Nicole knew she would be very happy here.

It was about 5:15 p.m. when they finished moving Nicole in. Though she and Alexander didn't mention their kiss, the remembrance of it hung between them like thick fog. Nicole was a nervous wreck every time he glanced at her and touched her—by mistake or on purpose, she wasn't sure.

"Hey, is anyone else hungry?" Victor asked as they all lounged in the living room after the last bags had been unloaded.

"I am," Monique answered from her perch on the arm of a chair.

"What about you two?" Victor smiled at Nicole and Alex, who purposefully sat a good distance apart on the sofa.

"I could eat," Nicole slowly admitted and inwardly groaned at the prospect of having to spend more tension-filled time in Alexander's maddening presence.

"Well, bro?" Victor stood and nudged Alex's shoulder. "Are you with us?"

All eyes fixated on him, and his locked with Nicole's uneasy ones.

"Sure." Alex finally sighed. "But nothing fancy."

"Dressed like this—" Victor glanced at their attire— "Casual is the way to go. How about the Latin Quarter?"

"Perfect." Monique walked over to the sofa. "Excuse us girls while we freshen up." She took Nicole's hand and pulled her up from the sofa and out of the room. Once they were alone in her bedroom, she turned to Nicole. "What's wrong? You look shell-shocked."

"Nothing's wrong."

"Are you nervous about going out with the boss?" Monique correctly surmised.

"No." At Monique's skeptical stare, she confessed, "Okay, yes. What am I supposed to say to him?"

"Oh, Nicole!" Monique laughed and gave her a light hug. "Victor and I will be there. Besides, he's simply a man—a rich, powerful, handsome man, but still just a man."

"He's also our boss."

"There's no law against having dinner with the boss," Monique reminded her.

"I suppose not." Nicole fingered her hair. "I really should be happy he's gotten over his displeasure with me for being a week late."

"I told you he'd get over it."

"I know, but I didn't expect it to happen so quickly," Nicole admitted. "He's so…"

"What? Appealing? Available?"

"No, unpredictable."

"Hasn't anyone ever told you predictability is boring?" Monique winked. "Come on, let's make ourselves presentable for our *dates,*" she said suggestively and laughed heartily at Nicole's uneasy expression at her choice of words.

Alexander glared at his brother, fighting the urge to punch him. Sometimes he wished he was an only child.

"You had to open your big mouth, didn't you?"

"What's wrong? Do you have something against having dinner with two beautiful women?"

"Nicole is probably tired and wants to relax," Alexander insisted. "She felt pressured into going because she didn't want to be rude."

"Are you sure you're not talking about yourself?" Victor asked.

"I helped her move, didn't I?"

"With some prodding from me." Alex rolled his eyes at Victor's self-satisfied expression and was rewarded by one of his brother's sheepish grins.

"More like nagging," Alex corrected.

"You owed her," Victor reminded. "We both did."

"Yeah, I know." Alex scratched his chin. "I'm not complaining."

"No? Then what do you call this?"

"Nothing." Alex ran a hand over his lips, which still longed for the taste of Nicole's. "Forget it."

* * *

Victor studied Alex's pensive expression. He knew his brother was definitely interested in Nicole, but he also knew, because of a horrible past relationship, Alex wouldn't risk cultivating that obvious interest—unless someone gave him a not-so-gentle shove in the right direction.

Well, he thought, chuckling inwardly, *that's what little brothers are for!*.

"Alex, what happened between you two in the bedroom?"

"Nothing," Alex quickly denied and shushed Victor's response when Nicole and Monique returned. "Ready?"

"Ready," Monique and Nicole responded in unison and then laughed.

"Then let's go." Victor opened the door and followed the ladies out, with his somber brother in tow.

The weather was still pleasant, with the temperature in the low sixties as they walked toward the Latin Quarter. Monique and Victor led the way, with Alex and Nicole following behind them.

The closer they got to the quarter, the more crowded the sidewalks became, and the streets narrowed, causing the two couples to gravitate toward each other. Somehow, Nicole wound up holding Alex's hand, and Monique hooked her hand through Victor's arm to keep from getting separated.

Each side of the narrow street was lined wall to wall with six-story grayish-white stone buildings. It was difficult to tell where one shop or bistro ended and another started. The streets were a little restrictive, but the carefree charm of the quarter soon took Nicole under its spell, and she glanced around with wide, excited eyes.

As they neared their destination, the festive music increased in tempo and volume, and suddenly it seemed as if all the inhabitants of the busy streets and sidewalks were talking and laughing at once, making it nearly impossible to hear the person standing right next to you. Victor ushered them into a crowded and boisterous bistro that he swore served the best pizza in town.

A makeshift dance floor was filled with revelers, and a table only became available after Alex discretely handed a waiter several folded bills. Even though they were four, they were seated at a small table for two, which meant they had to sit ridiculously close together—Nicole, to her delight and dismay, found herself pressed against Alexander on one side and Monique on the other.

"Isn't this a great place?" Victor asked.

"What?" Monique, Nicole and Alex screamed over the loud music.

"Isn't this nice?" Victor screamed back.

"It's great if we don't want to hear each other," Alex drily shouted.

"I like it," Nicole decided.

"Me, too," Monique chimed in.

"Well, since we can't hear each other—" Victor turned and smiled at Monique "—how about a dance?"

"Huh?" Monique leaned a little closer to him.

"A dance?" Victor stood and showed off a few moves. "How about it?"

"Oh." Monique laughed and then shocked everyone by standing and agreeing. "Why not?"

Victor nudged Alex's arm. "Don't just sit there, bro. Ask Nicole to dance."

"Thank you for the unsolicited advice, Victor." Alex glared. "Now get lost."

Victor chuckled, took Monique's hand and pulled her off toward the other dancers. Once alone, Nicole furtively glanced at Alex, who was watching her intensely.

Chapter 5

"Would you like to dance, Nicole?"

"No." She shook her head. "I'm fine, really."

"Come on." Alex stood and offered his hand. "I promise not to step on your toes."

This was a bad idea. She knew it was a bad idea; however, after only a second's hesitation, she took his hand and stood. It was only one dance. Where was the harm in that? *You know where the harm lies,* she silently chastised but ignored her wise advice.

The music was fast and loud. Nicole and Alexander made their way through the throng of people until they reached the dance floor. Smiling at each other a little uneasily, they began to dance. Soon Nicole was lost in the beat, and she and Alexander danced very well together. She was surprised at how good a dancer he was. The type of music didn't necessitate them touching much, but each was keenly aware of the other as their bodies teased and flirted.

When the song ended some minutes later, an unexpected slow one started. Alex and Nicole stared at each other before he extended his hand, which she slowly took and allowed herself to be drawn into his strong arms. Her free hand rested on his shoulder, and she swallowed a lump in her throat as their bodies nearly touched.

"Well, at least we can hear each other now." Alexander now spoke in near normal tones.

"Yes." Nicole wasn't sure if that was a plus or a minus.

"Nicole, about our kiss earlier." Alex broached the subject that hung thickly between them. "I'm sorry—"

"It's all right," she quickly interrupted. The last thing she wanted was for him to apologize for kissing her. "Let's just forget it."

"Can you do that?" He watched her closely.

"Of course." She forced herself to appear unconcerned, praying he would buy her carefully orchestrated lie. She wouldn't forget that kiss for a long time.

"It won't happen again."

At his easy assurance, she felt like asking him why not, but she refrained.

She purposefully changed subjects. "Have you been here before?"

"No. I come to the Quarter often, but there are so many shops and restaurants it's easy to miss one."

"I'll bet." She fought a groan as his hand moved across her lower back. "It's very festive. It reminds me of Mardi Gras in New Orleans."

"Ah, New Orleans." Alex smiled wistfully. "I haven't been to a Mardi Gras in years."

"Do you get back to the States regularly?" Lord, it was torture chitchatting when his nearness was making it impossible to think clearly.

"I try to make it once or twice a year for a few months." He smiled. "You're a good dancer, by the way."

"Thank you." She returned his smile. "I'd better be.

My sister, Natasha, is a prima ballerina, and she taught me how to dance."

"She did a wonderful job."

"She'll be happy to hear that." She laughed as he expertly twirled her around. "You're not too bad yourself."

"My mother insisted on sending me and Vic to dance class every Saturday." He rolled his eyes. "We hated it."

"What little boy wouldn't?" Nicole sympathized. "At least it paid off."

"I guess that is some consolation now, but back then…" He made a face, and Nicole laughed.

"Why do our parents insist on embarrassing us?"

"I have no idea." He paused thoughtfully and then offered, "I think it's embedded in their DNA."

"I think you're right."

They fell silent and concentrated on the seductive music, which seamlessly merged into another song, much to Nicole's dismay. It felt too good being in Alexander's arms; she wanted to entwine her arms around his neck, press closer to him and feel his lips on hers again. *Oh, God, what was she thinking?* She suddenly stepped out of his embrace, and he eyed her curiously but remained silent.

"We should go back to our table," she said, attempting to explain her actions. "Monique and Victor are probably looking for us."

"Think again." She followed his gaze and saw Monique and Victor still dancing.

He pulled her back into his arms, and they continued their dance. It felt good being in his arms, her soft body yielding against his hardness. She was content to simply dance with him all night. She longed for him to kiss her again—properly, thoroughly this time, the way he would have if Victor hadn't interrupted them.

"Alexander?"

"Hmm?" He focused on Nicole's questioning gaze, his eyes laced with barely concealed hunger.

"Where were you?"

"Just thinking."

"About?"

"Nothing in particular," he said, pulling her closer and resting his chin against the top of her head.

She would bet her life he had been thinking about their kiss, as she had. That delighted and dismayed her. They shouldn't be thinking about kissing each other; things were getting completely out of hand between them. He was her boss, not her date. The sudden stark realization that she longed for him to be the latter instead of the former caused her to pull back from his much-too-welcome embrace. She needed to put some distance between them—now!

"I'm thirsty." Nicole pushed fully out of his arms and walked back to the table without waiting for his response.

When she reached it, he was standing beside her, holding out her chair as she sat down. It was perfect timing because their drinks were being placed on the table. Nicole picked up her glass and took a long drink while Alex watched her as if she were an insect under a microscope.

"Mmm, that hit the spot," she said, mainly to have something to say.

Alex took a big gulp of his own drink. "Yeah, it sure does."

Nicole glanced around, feigning interest in the ambiance to escape his penetrating gaze. He remained silent, and she made the mistake of looking at him. His concentrated stare sucked all air from her lungs.

He shrugged out of his jacket and placed it on the back of his chair, thus ending Nicole's ability to concentrate on small talk. Her eyes were drawn to his powerful arms, left bare by the short-sleeved white T-shirt he wore. He was so ripped; he must work out.

Her wandering eyes continued exploring his magnificient physique, trailing from one shoulder to the next, lingering on his well-defined pecs pressing against the confines of his shirt. When her eyes rose to his face, he was again watching her with intense hunger that nearly sent her flying off her stool.

Before either of them could speak or react, Monique and Victor chose that moment to rejoin them, plopping down onto their respective seats in breathless laughter.

"Whew, that was fun!"

Victor's eyes twinkled. "Because I was your dance partner?"

"In spite of." Monique sipped her drink.

"Just can't give me a compliment." Victor grinned. "Can you?"

"No," Monique easily admitted.

Victor turned his attention to the other noticeably silent couple. "Alex didn't bruise your toes, did he Nicole?"

"No, I didn't." Alex shot Victor a killing look. "I do know how to dance with a woman, you know."

"I just thought you might be a little rusty, bro." Victor snickered at his brother's scowl.

Nicole watched the interplay between the brothers with interest. Much more than simple dancing was being discussed between them. Apparently Alexander hadn't been dating much lately, and for the life of her, she couldn't understand why. Frankly, a handsome man like him should have women beating down his door.

"Well, I'm not," Alex growled.

"He's definitely not," Nicole agreed, and Alexander shot her a private smile, which Victor and Monique intercepted. Thankfully, their pizza was delivered before they could remark on it.

"Just in time." Alex glared at his brother. "Maybe food will keep you quiet."

"Mmm, it looks wonderful." Nicole placed a napkin on her lap and prayed food would stem the need for awkward conversation.

"I know how to eat and talk at the same time," Victor said slyly.

"God, help us." Alex's audible sigh had everyone laughing.

"Here, chew on this." Monique placed a gooey piece of pizza on Victor's plate.

"I thought you were going to feed me?"

"Dream on," Monique scoffed.

"Dreaming is my middle name," Victor promised with a wink.

"I swear he was adopted." Alex shook his head in mock disgust. Victor stuck out his tongue at his brother, and Nicole and Monique nearly choked on their pizza from laughter.

As Victor had predicted, it was the best pizza they had ever eaten. Dinner passed amicably enough, with an occasional good-natured barb directed at Alex or Monique from Victor, and then they made their way back to Monique and Nicole's place. They congregated outside of the apartment door in preparation of calling it a night.

"Thanks for dinner and for helping me move." Nicole directed her gratitude toward Alexander.

"It was our pleasure," Alex responded before Victor could.

"Yes, thank you, guys." Monique glanced from Alex to Nicole, who seemed to only have eyes for each other.

"You're welcome." Victor spoke up when it was obvious Alex hadn't heard a word Monique said. "We'll have to do this again sometime—the dinner part, I mean."

"We'll see," Monique noncommittally responded.

"Well, good night ladies." Alex tore his eyes away from

Nicole, took his brother's arm and pulled him away. "See you at work tomorrow."

"Good night," Nicole and Monique echoed before entering their apartment.

"Why the hasty exit, Alex?"

"They were ready for us to go." Truthfully, he was ready to go before he did something unwise—like kiss Nicole again in front of everyone.

"It didn't seem that way to me," Victor argued. "I think I made some progress with Monique tonight."

Alex raised an eyebrow. "Are you interested in her?"

Victor shrugged. "I wouldn't mind dating her."

"Oh, no you don't!" Alex stopped and slapped his brother across the back of the head.

"Ouch!" Victor grumbled, rubbing his head. "What's that for?"

"Listen, you. Good designers are hard to come by. So don't you mess with mine unless you're contemplating *marriage.*"

"Yes, sir!" Victor saluted, and Alex's frown intensified.

"I mean it, Victor."

"Alex, it's called *casual* dating, and there's no law against it." Victor sighed. "You need to get out more, bro."

"I get out every day."

"You know what I mean. How long has it been since you had a date with a lady that I didn't force you to go on?"

"You know exactly how long it's been. Five years."

"Nina wasn't a lady. She was a barracuda," Victor insisted.

Alex couldn't disagree with that. At the mention of a woman he wanted to forget, his eyes hardened perceptibly, and tension rolled off him in waves.

"I don't want to talk about Nina."

"I know, bro." Victor patted his stiff shoulder. "Lord knows I don't blame you for that after what she pulled."

"Change subjects, Vic," Alex demanded and started walking again.

"Okay." Victor held up his hands in surrender and followed. "Nicole is nice, isn't she?"

"Yes." He wasn't too sure he liked this subject either.

"You're attracted to her."

"I hardly know her."

"But you'd like to." Victor stared at his rigid profile. "Wouldn't you?"

"I don't date my employees, Victor."

"You used to." His unpleasant reminder caused a thinning of Alex's lips.

"Which is exactly why I don't anymore."

"Alex, you can't judge every woman by *she who shall be nameless*." Victor gave his shoulder a shake. "Leave the past where it belongs."

Alex sighed heavily. "Easy for you to say."

"I know, but you can't keep living like a monk, man."

"I'm not."

"Oh, no?" Victor stopped walking, forcing Alex to do the same. "When was the last time you…?"

Alex's frown halted his words. "Victor, I don't intend to talk about my sex life with you."

"Because you don't have one." At his brother's darkening countenance and clenched fists, he took a step back and chuckled in mock surrender. "Okay, okay, I can take a hint."

"Since when?"

"Since I just remembered you're slightly bigger than me and that you fight dirty." Alex laughed at his assertion, as intended.

"Tell yourself whatever you have to in order to explain

the fact that I can still whip your butt," Alex said as they started walking again.

"I just have respect for my elders." Victor grinned. "That's all."

"Whatever you say, Vic. Whatever you say." Alex placed an arm around his shoulder as they walked off, laughing companionably.

Neither of them spoke, each lost in their own secret thoughts. Alex silently admitted Victor was right; he was attracted to Nicole—but he wasn't going to act on that attraction for a multitude of reasons. Most of all for his own self-preservation.

"Tonight was fun, wasn't it?" Monique smiled at Nicole as they sat side by side on the sofa.

"Yes, it was nice of Alexander and Victor to help me move. Did you ask them to do that?"

"No, I was as surprised as you were." Monique paused before offering, "I think the boss likes you."

"Don't be ridiculous!" Nicole's words came out more forceful than intended. "I mean…"

"So you like him, too." Monique's smile showed that she approved.

"I just met him," Nicole said to evade the question. "Besides, he's my boss."

"What do either of those things have to do with it?" Monique shrugged dismissively. "This is Paris, the city of love—not New York. In this country, employees date their bosses and don't think anything of it."

"Perhaps, but I'm not going to date Alexander. That's not why I'm here."

"We'll see." Monique tucked her legs underneath her. "Chemistry is a powerful force to fight."

Nicole completely agreed.

"I'm beat." Nicole suddenly stood. "I think I'll take a shower and turn in."

"Tired of my unsolicited advice, huh?"

"No, I'm just exhausted. It's been a long day."

"It has indeed." Monique stretched her arms above her head and then smiled. "I'm glad you're here, Nicole."

"Me, too." She bent down, kissed her roomie's cheek and walked toward her room. "Good night," she said over her shoulder.

"Good night," Monique echoed with a broad smile.

Nicole entered her bathroom and closed the door. About thirty minutes later, after a long relaxing bath during which forbidden thoughts of Alexander tortured her, she went to her room, donned a black T-shirt two sizes too large and climbed into her inviting bed.

She sighed contentedly as the mattress conformed to her body and the white down comforter caressed her nearly bare skin. Her head sank into the pillow as she turned onto her back and stared up at the ceiling. A soft cool breeze ruffled the sheer white curtains at her window, and she inhaled happily.

Her overactive imagination refused to be muted. She tried to keep her mind from fixating on Alexander, but she failed miserably. He was so mysterious, unpredictable and kind. Why did he have to be so appealing? Why couldn't he be obnoxious and unlikeable? At first she had thought that description fit him perfectly, but she now knew he was as far from that unflattering description as he was from being untalented.

Oh, God, why did he have to kiss her? The brevity of it had only made her long for more, and she wondered how she was going to face him at work in the morning without her mind torturing her with the memory of how his lips had felt against hers.

Her body masochistically reminded her brain of the

short yet vivid time it had spent in close proximity to Alexander's as they had slow danced; her flesh still tingled as if his body had been permanently imprinted on hers. She still felt his big hands nearly engulfing hers and resting on her waist.

Closing her eyes, she remembered how the muscular shoulders and chest seemed ready to escape the confines of his shirt when he had removed his jacket. She wondered if his chest and abdomen were covered with the same fine black hairs that dusted his forearms. A smile curved her lips before she placed a hand to her mouth, horrified at her thoughts.

"This is all your fault, Marcy," she grumbled and then chuckled at the thought of her new sister-in-law.

Nathan and Marcy were on their honeymoon. When they returned in a few weeks, she'd have to call Marcy and complain that her teasing about Paris's romantic ambience casting a spell on her was coming true. Nicole was determined to fight the pull of attraction she felt toward Alexander with everything she had; however, after tonight, she wondered if she possessed enough resolve to be successful in that endeavor.

Sighing, she turned onto her side and stared out the window. She had no intention of jeopardizing a wonderful career opportunity by unwisely incorporating a romantic entanglement into the mix. Alexander had gotten over her being late, she had made two good friends and had moved in with one, she was codesigning a gown with one of the best designers in the world and it was going to be featured in his next fashion show.

Her career was going fabulously, and she wasn't going to jeopardize it for anything, especially not for a brief fling. She'd get her attraction to Alexander under control soon—somehow.

That decided, she stifled a yawn with the back of her

hand. She was exhausted but happy to be in her bed in her new home instead of a hotel. She was going to be happy here; she felt it. Plumping her pillows, she turned onto her stomach, closed her eyes and told herself to go to sleep.

It didn't take long for sleep to claim her. However, against her will, her last thoughts centered on the man who was off-limits to her—the enigmatic Alexander James.

Chapter 6

Nicole hummed happily as she entered the break room to make herself a morning cup of coffee. She was stirring in cream when the door opened. She glanced around with a smile, which fell from her mouth as she recognized Crystal—the woman who had yet to say ten whole words to her.

"Good morning," Nicole brightly greeted, deciding to try to be friends with the woman determined to be her enemy.

"Well, well, if it isn't the new protégé."

Nicole's eyebrow rose at her snarky comment. "I beg your pardon?"

"The boss's new toy," Crystal vindictively substituted.

"Crystal." Nicole sat her china cup down in its matching saucer with a clank and turned to face the other woman. "Right?"

"Yes." She nearly hissed the word.

"Crystal, I'm Nicole." She offered her hand, which, as

expected, was blatantly ignored, so she shrugged and withdrew it. "We don't really know each other, so I'm at a loss to understand your hostility toward me."

"Nina was my friend," Crystal woodenly informed her.

"Who?"

"Nina Laurent," Crystal huffed. "The designer you're *trying* to replace."

"First of all, I've never heard of Nina Laurent, and second, I'm not trying to replace anyone. I was hired as Alexander's new designer." She paused, then continued. "Nina doesn't work here anymore, so I suggest you get used to that fact."

"Smug, aren't you?"

"It would be great if we could be professional, but that's up to you." Nicole picked up her coffee and walked toward the door. "I'd like to have a civil working relationship with you, but you'll have to meet me halfway." She paused, hoping her offer would sink in before promising, "I'm not going anywhere." Without a backward glance, she left the room.

Nicole had just settled back in at her desk after that run-in when Alexander entered the room. He stopped by several desks to look at a design, ask a question or answer one as he made his way toward her. Oh, boy, how should she act after their dance last night?

Good Lord, woman. It was just a dance—well, three—and you weren't on a date. You were out with his brother and your roommate.

She studied him as he approached. He wore a three-quarter-length black jacket, black shirt and black pants. Whew, he looked good! From the entourage of female eyes that followed him as he moved through the room, every lady present shared her sentiments. Unwilling to be caught staring, she quickly averted her head when he glanced her way, praying he hadn't seen her gawking at him.

Of course, he stopped at her desk, standing to the side of the tall stool on which she sat. He didn't say anything— simply watched her pretending to sketch. She tried to act normal, but after a few tense minutes, her hand began to shake, and she placed her charcoal onto the easel and turned to stare at him.

"Did you want something, Alexander?" She was proud that her voice didn't shake.

"Just observing," he responded. "Continue."

She picked up her charcoal again, blew out her breath from between her lips and willed herself to forget how close his maddening body was to hers as he watched her sketch. Her traitorous mind tortured her with memories of how wonderful it felt brushing against his hardness when they had danced last night.

"Thank you for helping me move."

"You're welcome."

She glanced at him sideways. "I enjoyed dinner."

"Did you?"

"Yes." She frowned slightly. "Didn't you?"

"Mmm-hmm," he noncommittally replied.

She nearly jumped out of her skin when his hand unexpectedly covered hers. He inhaled deeply, and was it her imagination or did his hand grip hers a little tighter? When she glanced at him, she felt like a tasty treat he couldn't wait to devour. She quickly lowered her eyes and willed her heart to cease its erratic pounding, as if it was trying to escape and lay itself at Alexander's feet in offering.

"Relax," he whispered into her ear, causing a shudder within her. "Your design is good, but how about making the sleeve more flowing?" His hand guided hers over the canvas. "Like this." Together they redesigned the sleeve; it was the sweetest torture. His free hand rested lightly on her shoulder, sliding down her arm before leaving her skin. "What do you think?"

"About what?" she whispered. *Had he been talking to her? She hadn't heard a word he said.*

"The design." He tapped the easel and released her hand.

"Oh." She swallowed her embarrassment and glanced at it. "Oh, yes, I see what you mean." She actually did when she glanced at the blouse, noting that the sleeve had been reshaped into a more blouson design instead of the tailored one she had been sketching.

"Good." He scratched his chin thoughtfully and suggested, "Why don't you try an empire waist, too?"

"Thank you for the suggestions." She inhaled deeply the spicy, clean male scent of him.

"You're welcome. You're very talented, Nicole," he praised and then walked away before she could respond.

Her confused gaze followed Alexander's retreating back for a few seconds before Nicole swung her eyes in the direction of Monique's office. That was a mistake because she immediately encountered Monique's smiling countenance through the glass wall.

Monique's smile widened as Nicole visibly sighed. She didn't have to say a word; Nicole knew what she was thinking—that she was attracted to Alexander. Unfortunately, it was the truth. Giving Monique a brief nod, she swiveled her chair around and glanced unseeingly at her sketch.

For a second she wondered if Alexander got off on disrupting the balance in her life. She brought a hand to her heart and willed it to slow down. She had to stop entertaining inappropriate thoughts about him, but that was proving next to impossible to accomplish.

As anticipated, Monique exited her office a few seconds later and perched on Nicole's desk. Nicole glanced up at her friend, who was still smiling.

"What?" Nicole asked as Monique remained blaringly silent.

"How's it going?"

"Good."

"What did the boss want?" Monique twirled a pencil between her fingers.

"He was just making a few suggestions about my design." Nicole paused before adding firmly, "That's all."

"He's a very hands-on boss," Monique couldn't resist adding. "Especially with you."

"That's nonsense." Nicole crossed her legs. "In case you didn't notice, mine wasn't the only desk he stopped at."

"That's true, but he spent more time with you," Monique smugly observed.

"Maybe he thinks I need more guidance than the other designers."

"I doubt it. I think he simply wanted to see you." Monique chuckled at Nicole's exasperated sigh and couldn't resist adding, "You two look so good together."

"Monique, how many times do I have to tell you I'm here to work and nothing else?"

"It seems I'm going to have to speak to Crystal and lay down the law."

Nicole blinked rapidly at Monique's unexpected change in subject and followed her friend's frowning gaze to where Crystal sat staring at them pointedly. After a few seconds, Crystal lowered her head to her drawing and began scribbling furiously.

"No, don't do that," Nicole said. "I spoke with her earlier. I tried to be friends with her." Nicole shrugged. "But she resents me trying to take Nina Laurent's place." She watched Monique closely, who stiffened noticeably at the mention of the name. "Did you know Nina?"

"Yes." Heretofore laughing eyes grew hooded.

"What's the story about her?"

"Short and sweet, she was disloyal and was fired."

"That really is short." Nicole studied her friend closely. "I'm sure there's much more to it than that."

"There is, but it's not my story to tell." Monique stood. "Now, I'll let you get back to work."

A frown marred Nicole's expression as she wondered whose story it was. Instinctively, she knew the answer— it was Alexander's.

One thing Nicole could say about Alexander James—he wasn't a liar. For the next two weeks he worked her mercilessly, and she was happy to say that she had stood up very well under the pressure. Neither of them mentioned their kiss again, and she tried to forget it as he obviously had—a fact that slightly annoyed her, even though she knew it was for the best.

Finally, it was the weekend; this was her first and last Saturday off before they would go to a six-day workweek to get ready for Alexander's spring fashion show. Nicole intended to make the most of it by going sightseeing until she dropped.

Dressed in black jeans, a white sleeveless sweater, a black leather jacket and black walking boots, she carried a large black hobo bag she planned to stuff with purchases. First, she had to make a quick stop at the office to pick up her tablet.

It was a little after 9:00 a.m. when she walked into Alexander's and made her way up to the sixth floor and her workstation. Grabbing her tablet, she turned to leave and nearly collided with Alex in the process. He was dressed casually in faded jeans and a gray long-sleeved pullover shirt.

"Jesus!" She placed a hand to her heart. "You enjoy sneaking up on me, don't you?"

"I wasn't sneaking," Alex denied around a smile. "It's your day off. What are you doing here?"

"I'm on my way to do the tourist thing—sightseeing—but first I wanted to stop by and pick this up." Nicole held up the tablet in her hands before placing it in her bag. "Are you working today?"

"No, just came in to take a look at some fabric samples."

"I'll let you get back to it." As she walked around him, his hand on her arm halted her. She glanced at him questioningly.

"Would you like a guide?"

Her eyes widened in surprise. "You?"

"Yes." His eyes shone teasingly. "Won't I do?"

He would do just fine; that was the problem. She was trying to stay away from him unless it had to do with business, and she had thus far been successful.

"Of course you'll do, but no thank you," she politely declined. "I just want to take my time, walk around by myself and absorb the history and culture of the city."

She frowned when he began chuckling, which quickly changed into a full-blown laugh. It was a pleasing sound, but she resented it being directed at her when she didn't understand why.

"What's so funny?" Her frown grew as he fought to unsuccessfully control his laughter. She placed her hands on her hips. "Well?"

After wiping his eyes, he managed to say through chuckles, "Are you an *I Love Lucy* fan?"

"What does that have to do with anything?"

"Are you?" he persisted.

"Yes."

"Well, do you remember the episode when the gang was in Paris and Lucy insisted on going sightseeing by herself?"

Understanding finally dawned on Nicole. "She ended up in jail facing counterfeiting charges."

"Exactly." He chuckled again. "I'd hate for that to happen to you."

"So would I." She laughed. "I can't believe you're a *Lucy* fan."

"Isn't everyone?"

"If they're not, they should be," she professed.

"I couldn't agree more. They don't make shows like that anymore."

"Nope, today everything is reality television." She screwed up her nose in distaste.

"Come on now, some reality shows are okay."

"Maybe one or two," she relented. "But nothing can touch *Lucy*. Whenever there's a marathon, I wind up in front of the television for hours laughing until my sides hurt," Nicole confessed.

"Me, too. What's your favorite episode?"

"That's a hard question. How could you choose?" Her brows furrowed in thought. "One of my favorites is the 'Bonus Buck' episode." She chuckled as scenes flashed in her head. "That laundry scene is a classic."

"Oh, yeah." Alex grinned. "Remember the very last scene when Lucy comes into the newspaper office after falling into the starch vat? That's priceless."

"Oh, God, that was so funny." Nicole chuckled and added, "Her cheeks were sunken and her lips were puckered, and her hair…" She dissolved into giggles.

"And after they paid for all the damages out of the winnings, all they had left was a dollar." They both shared a laugh before getting control of themselves again.

"So," Alex said, smiling disarmingly, "are you going to take me up on my offer, or risk going about by yourself?"

She knew she should refuse, but she didn't want to. The idea of exploring Paris with him appealed to her very much. Besides, where was the harm in spending a few hours in broad daylight in a crowded city with him?

"If you're sure…"

"I am."

"Okay, I'm all yours." At his darkening eyes and sexy smile, she hastily amended, "For today…for sightseeing."

God, somebody please pull my big foot out of my run-away mouth!

His smile widened as they walked out into the hallway. She waited while he retrieved his leather jacket from his office, and then they entered the elevator and were soon walking out of the building into the cool sunshine.

"Walk or ride?"

"Although I'd love another spin in that wicked car of yours, I had my heart set on walking today."

"You think my car is wicked, huh?"

"Totally," she assured as they started walking.

"I'll have to take you for a ride outside of the city and show you what she can really do."

"She's pretty awesome in the city."

"Yeah, but on the open road—" he sighed happily "—she's magic." He glanced at her. "So what did you want to visit today? The Eiffel tower? The Sorbonne?"

"I want to see those places, but since today's Saturday, I'm sure they're crowded. I had planned on walking around and seeing where my feet lead me."

"That's probably wise," Alex agreed as they walked slowly down the sidewalk in silence for a while.

"You and Victor seem very close," Nicole said, finally breaking the silence.

"Yeah, we are. That nut's my best friend."

"I must confess I look forward to his visits to the office." Alex glanced at her and frowned.

"Why?" Lord, he hoped she wasn't going to pump him for info on his brother!

"Because it's obvious how much you love each other."

He must have looked uneasy because she asked, "Uh-oh, did I embarrass you?"

He chuckled. "No."

"Are you sure? I know how guys get about admitting their feelings."

"You didn't embarrass me," he reiterated. To prove his point, he continued with the same topic of conversation. "Vic and I have always been close—a bond that intensified five years ago when our parents died."

"I'm sorry."

"Thanks." They walked in silence, then he asked, "Don't you want to know what happened to them?"

"Plane crash," she quickly answered. "Right?"

"How…?" He smiled at her rueful expression and answered his unfinished question. "Internet?"

"Yes, and fashion magazines and news reports." She shrugged apologetically. "I'm a fashion junkie, and you're my favorite designer."

His face registered shock. "I am?"

"Mmm-hmm." She laughed at his surprise.

"Why?"

"Why? Lots of reasons. I love your fresh, new, innovative style. Plus, you design classic with a twist better than anyone I've ever seen. Your Maltino collection last year was pure genius," she gushed.

"Thanks for the praise, but I'm not sure I deserve it."

"Believe me, you do. You're a genius."

"You're too kind." Her words affected him deeply because he could tell she really meant them. She wasn't trying to kiss up to him or get in his good graces like so many others had before her.

"I mean it," she said with a smile. "Thank you for allowing me to be a part of Alexander's. It's a dream come true for me."

"We're lucky to have you." He softly touched her cheek. "I really mean that, Nicole."

"Now *you're* being too kind," she whispered.

"No, I'm being honest."

Of their own volition, his fingers trailed across her soft skin as if mesmerized by its smooth texture. His eyes followed the journey of his fingers, and he felt rather than saw her quickly indrawn breath. His eyes slowly rose to meet hers, and they both realized they were a hairbreadth away from once again crossing that forbidden line between them that suddenly seemed meaningless and inconsequential.

Chapter 7

They stared at each other, telegraphing silent forbidden messages until he broke eye contact. Things had suddenly turned from lighthearted to extremely personal, and he needed to dispel the dangerous intimacy that had too quickly developed between them.

"How about a walk on the Pont Neuf Bridge and then a ride on an excursion boat? It will give us a great tour of the banks of the Seine River, and you'll also get a close-up look at some of Paris's famous bridges. The boat loading dock is some distance from here, though. We can take the train, bus, my car or a taxi," he suggested.

"Let's walk." She silently willed her skin to stop tingling from his touch.

"Walking it is."

The coolness of the morning made the walk pleasant and easy. Alexander showed her points of interest along the way, stopping when she wanted to get a closer look at something and answering any questions she had with a smile and with expert knowledge that amazed her; he was like a walking tour book.

All too soon they reached their destination of the first district. They made their way over the Pont des Arts pedestrian bridge, which crossed the Seine River. Even at this early hour, the bridge was already bustling with people scurrying to and fro.

"That's the Institut de France." Alex pointed to the end of the bridge on which they walked, where a huge conglomerate of stone buildings stood, highlighted by a center building with an ornate dome. "We can tour some of the museums after the boat ride if you'd like."

"That would be great."

Soon they reached the loading ramp for the white metal excursion boat. It was completely open, without solid walls, two decks and a roof made of steel bars. They stood along the side and leaned against the rails. The breeze blew her bangs into her eyes, and without thinking, Alex brushed them away and trailed his fingers across her forehead and slowly down her cheek.

She held her breath, and he suddenly dropped his hand and started pointing out landmarks. She only half listened, wanting only one thing at the moment—for Alexander to kiss her. She wondered if he wanted the same. He seemed completely in control as he continued relating facts about their surroundings, which she had to struggle to comprehend.

"Nicole?"

"Hmm?"

"Am I boring you?" Alexander's question jolted her out of her forbidden thoughts, and she glanced at him guiltily.

"No, of course not." She silently scolded herself to pay attention. "Please continue."

"Are you sure?" At her nod, he resumed, "Okay. I was

saying the Seine River is 482 miles long. It's an important commercial waterway for the Paris Basin in north France."

"One thing I love most about Paris is seeing water nearly everywhere I look." Nicole's gaze skirted over the blue waves. "It reminds me of home."

"I couldn't agree more. I think that's one of the reasons I like it so much." He pointed off in the distance. "There are thirty-seven bridges in Paris and tons more for the length of the river outside the city. Pont Neuf means 'new bridge,' but the Neuf is actually the oldest bridge across the Seine. It was completed in 1607."

"You're very knowledgeable."

"I've lived here most of my life, and I enjoy learning about this city's rich history."

"I'm enjoying it, too. Listening to you certainly beats reading a guide book. Keep going," Nicole ordered, and he laughed.

"Let me see." He tapped his clean-shaven chin thoughtfully, a quirk she found appealing. "Outside the city limits, you'll find the Pont de Normandie, one of the longest cable-stayed bridges in the world, which links Le Havre to Honfleur."

"I'd love to see that."

"Well, when we finish here…"

Nicole glanced curiously at Alexander when he stopped speaking and found him staring at a man suddenly standing on his right.

Without them realizing it, an ever-growing crowd of people had gathered around them, listening intently to Alex as he imparted a bit of history to Nicole. The official tour guide glanced pointedly at them.

"It seems we have an audience," Nicole stated.

"Uh-oh," Alex whispered. "This reminds me of another *Lucy* episode."

"Don't tell me—'The Tour Bus?'" Nicole correctly guessed.

"Yep." Alex grinned. They stared at each other, trying to suppress it, but companionable laughter burst forth.

The crowd watched the laughing couple, trying to understand their private joke. The tour guide grew more impatient with them by the second and didn't bother to hide his annoyance.

"Sir...mademoiselle..."

"I apologize." Alex interrupted the guide and, taking Nicole's hand, pulled her to the other side of the boat where they were relatively alone.

"You're going to get us kicked off," Nicole good-naturedly complained.

"Can you swim?"

"I can."

"I hope it doesn't come to that." He leaned his hip against the rail. "But that's good to know."

"Just so you know." Nicole leaned forward and whispered, "I enjoyed your facts much more than the guide's."

"Thanks." Alex chuckled. "He was really mad, wasn't he?"

"I think he was." She furtively glanced at the frowning guide. "Correction—he still is."

"I'm sorry about that, but I can't help it that the other people found me interesting."

"They have good taste," Nicole said.

"Yeah?"

"Oh, yes," Nicole solemnly vowed.

He could have said a lot—a lot she could have said, too—but they both remained silent and turned to stare out at the choppy blue water in companionable silence.

Alex made it a point to keep further commentary for Nicole's ears only, thus ensuring they weren't thrown off the boat prematurely. After the two-hour boat ride, they toured the first, second and third districts before going to the fifth and finally the sixth. Along the way, Nicole did some shopping, and she was surprised that Alexander didn't seem the least bit impatient as she explored one shop after another for several hours.

In one store she fell in love with a colorful porcelain carousel music box. She hesitated over whether or not to buy it. Alexander encouraged her to get it and even went so far as to offer to get it for her, which she quickly refused. In the end, she left her treasure in the store window because she had bought so much already.

"Let's walk down to the Luxembourg Gardens," Alex suggested when they entered the 6th Arrondisement.

"Sounds good."

A short while later they entered the Gardens. Nicole had never seen anything so beautiful in her life.

"Well…" Alex watched her with a smile. "What do you think?"

"This is…" She spread her hands in awe. "This is the most beautiful sight I've ever seen." He smiled at her genuine delight as she glanced around. "It's gorgeous."

"It's something, isn't it?"

"Wow," she gushed and he laughed, taking her hand in his as they walked down the long winding concrete walkway that was littered with people, some sitting on the side near the green grass in chairs, others walking and chatting.

Tall trees were blossoming. Gravel and colored flowers were arranged in various patterns, and Nicole lost count of the innumerable statues and huge fountains.

"This is the second largest public park in Paris. I come here a lot to unwind and think." He took her hand as they walked on.

"I can see why." She glanced around appreciatively. "It's so peaceful."

"With all the people constantly visiting, you wouldn't think it would be, but it is a very calming place."

They walked on with Nicole trying to take in every point of interest, but it was impossible. They passed a large fenced-in playground where young children and their parents were having a ball enjoying a vintage carousel.

"This is called the garden of the Senate," Alex said. "The Senate itself is housed in the Luxembourg Palace." He pointed to a huge brick complex flanked by tailored lawns and beautiful shrubs, flowers, more sculptures, bushes and trees. It was both regal and welcoming, and people milled about taking pictures, sitting in chairs relaxing or reading plaques of useful information.

"Wow." Nicole breathed in wonder and then laughed. "I guess I should expand my vocabulary."

"You're perfect the way you are."

"Thanks." Her voice was breathless because all air left her lungs at his sincere compliment. With a kind word, he could turn her into putty.

"The southwest corner contains apple and pear orchards and a puppet theater."

"I've got to see the orchards," Nicole decided.

"Your wish is my command." Alex guided her in the right direction.

They spent several hours touring the gardens and had barely scratched the surface when they left the grounds at 4:30 p.m. Where had the day gone? She had spent it in the company of a fascinating man who made her forget about everything.

"Are you hungry?"

"I'm starved."

"You should be. We haven't eaten all day," Alex said. "I know this little place close by where they serve the best snails."

At his serious delivery, Nicole did a double take. "Snails?"

"Don't worry, I'll make sure they serve them with plenty of ketchup." He winked and laughed. After a second's hesitation, she joined him, realizing he was joking.

"You really are a *Lucy* fan, aren't you?"

"I told you I was."

"I believe you after today." She automatically took his offered hand. "Where are we going?"

"To the Café de Flore. It's not far from your place." At the touch of her skin against his, the hunger he felt for food was crushed by blinding desire for her luscious lips. "Have you been there?"

"No, not yet. I've been meaning to go, though."

"There's no time like the present," he proclaimed.

They reached the famous art deco sidewalk café located at the corner of Boulevard Saint-Germain and Rue St. Benoit in no time. Luckily, they found an outside table under the white awning. They shared a bottle of wine while they decided what to order.

"Parisians have wine at all times of the day." Nicole raised her glass to her lips.

He leaned forward and whispered, "You're over twenty-one, right?"

"Safely over twenty-one," she promised.

"Good." He sat back, stretched out his legs and crossed his ankles. "Did you enjoy your tour?"

"Are you kidding?" She stared at him in surprise. "I've had a wonderful time today."

"Me, too," he admitted, fingers absently tracing the rim of his glass. "Actually, this was the most relaxing Saturday I've had in a long time."

"I'm glad." Nicole raised her glass in a toast. "You've been a wonderful tour guide and great company."

"Thanks." He touched his glass to hers.

"So what's good here?"

"Everything." He grinned. "Even the snails."

"Um, I think I'll pass on those." She stuck out her tongue, and he chuckled.

They settled on steak sandwiches, French fries and garden salad. The wonderful smells coming from nearby tables and the inside of the café were pure torture while they waited for their food to be prepared and delivered. When it was, they both dug in with appreciative gusto. They made occasional small talk as they polished off their meal.

Nicole plopped her last French fry into her mouth and sighed in contentment. She glanced up and found Alexander smiling at her.

"What? Do I have something on my face?"

"No, nothing." His smile widened as she placed a forkful of salad into her mouth. "I like a woman who doesn't play with her food."

"One thing my momma—who is a fabulous cook—taught me was to appreciate the food that's put in front of me because a lot of people aren't so fortunate."

"Very true."

"Besides." She glanced at her clean plate. "I love good food—I really do."

"Then you've definitely moved to the right place."

"Or the wrong place." She placed a hand on her now full stomach. "If I'm not careful, I'm going to gain twenty pounds. In fact, I think I'm well on my way."

"You look terrific."

"Thanks." They stared at each other and endured another uncomfortable silence, with Nicole contemplating forbidden thoughts about Alex.

After paying the bill, Alex cleared his throat and asked, "So what do you have planned for tonight?"

She considered admitting the truth—that she had nothing concrete planned and would be open to anything he suggested as long as it meant spending more time alone with him. It was insane how much she didn't want their time together to end. She was dangerously close to forgetting he was her boss.

"Monique said something about catching a movie," she finally answered.

"I'm sure you two will have fun."

"Well." She slowly stood, prompting Alexander to do the same. "I guess I should get going."

"Walk you home?"

"No, you don't need to do that."

"I don't mind." He picked up her bag, which was stuffed with her shopping purchases. "Besides, this is pretty heavy."

"This is nothing. You should see me when I really get going." She took her bag and easily slung it over her shoulder. "You've already given up your Saturday to show me around, and I really appreciate it."

"It was no hardship, Nicole."

"I'm glad." She impulsively kissed his cheek, close to the corner of his mouth. "Thank you for a wonderful day."

"You're welcome." His eyes darkened at her actions, but his voice remained steady. "Enjoy the rest of your weekend."

"You, too." She slowly backed away from temptation.

"See you Monday."

"Bright and early," she promised, turned and walked away while she still could.

With great effort, Nicole kept walking, wondering at the sense of loss she felt with each step she took away from Alexander. She sensed he was watching her, but she didn't dare turn around to find out. She needed to quickly get out of his presence and remind herself that he was her boss and not a man she liked, was attracted to and wanted to get to know better.

"Help me, Lord," she whispered, glancing heavenward, seeking divine guidance out of the sticky situation she had unwittingly gotten herself into where Alexander was concerned.

Chapter 8

"Hi," Monique greeted from her perch on the sofa as Nicole entered the living room and plopped down beside her. "Tired?"

"Happily exhausted." Nicole dropped her full purse to the floor.

"I take it the sightseeing went well."

"Oh, yes." Nicole's eyes grew dreamy. "We had a fabulous time."

"We?"

Nicole quickly glanced at Monique. Oh, darn, had she said *we?* "I…um…"

"Come on, give." Monique sat up at attention. "Who did you go with?"

Nicole hesitated before reluctantly admitting, "Alexander."

"Well, well," Monique drawled. "Fate seems to be bringing you two together."

"It was just an unplanned outing, Monique."

"Some of the best times I've had have been unplanned." Monique chuckled. "Did you have fun?"

"Yes, I did."

"Don't sound so surprised. You two have real chemistry."

"Oh, Monique!" Nicole tucked her feet beneath her. "Why do I have to be so attracted to our boss?" She shook her head helplessly and emphatically reiterated, "*Our boss!* What am I going to do?"

"How would you feel if you had to leave Paris tonight and knew you would never see him again?"

Nicole gasped at Monique's completely out-of-the-blue question.

"I'd miss my job, you and all of my new friends," she carefully answered.

"That wasn't the question." Monique gently shook her arm.

"Okay, I'd miss him." That was an understatement. She couldn't imagine not seeing Alexander again. How had this happened so quickly? "I don't want to jeopardize my career, but…"

"You'd like to date the boss," Monique finished for her.

"I think I would," Nicole tentatively admitted and then buried her head in her hands. "Oh, this is so wrong!"

"No, it's not." Monique pulled her hands away from her face. "Honey, life is too short to waste an opportunity. That's all I'm saying."

"I know it is," Nicole softly agreed. "But this is complicated."

"Most complications we create ourselves," Monique offered.

Nicole silently agreed, resting her head on the back of the sofa as she stared thoughtfully at the white ceiling, contemplating her worrisome attraction to Alexander and how to best handle it.

* * *

Alex entered his sprawling, secluded two-story brick house in the 16th district, whistling a bright tune. He dropped his keys on an oak table beside the door and rifled through the mail in his hands.

"You're in a good mood." Victor walked out of the kitchen holding a bottle of beer in one hand and a sandwich in the other.

"Hey, Vic." He glanced up and smiled at his brother. "What are you doing here—besides raiding my fridge?"

"I stopped by to see what you're up to." Victor took a bite of his sandwich.

"Nothing much." Alex shrugged out of his jacket, patted his brother on the back and walked into the living room with Victor trailing behind. "Just enjoying this great day."

"Wow, you really are in a good mood," Victor reiterated as they sat on side-by-side brown leather recliners.

"Is there a law against that?" Alex stretched out his legs and smiled.

"No, definitely not. It's good to see you smiling and happy."

"Thanks." It was good to feel happy, which he silently admitted he owed to Nicole. He felt alive around her.

"The question is, *why* are you smiling and happy?" Victor took a drink of his beer.

Alex shrugged as if he didn't know the reason. "Things are just going well—business is great, and…"

"You've met Nicole," Victor intuitively finished when Alex paused.

"She's very talented."

Victor bobbed his eyebrows. "How talented?"

"In fashion design, Victor." Alex sighed in disgust. "Get your mind out of the gutter."

"Sorry bro, no can do." Victor's quick denial received a chuckle from his brother. "Well?"

"Well what?"

Victor waved his hand. "What do you intend to do about Nicole and you getting together, and I mean that in the biblical sense."

"Victor, how many times do I have to tell you I'm not going down that road again? Just because we went sightseeing today…"

"Whoa, what?" Victor's eyes widened in surprise. "You went sightseeing with Nicole?"

"Yes," Alex reluctantly admitted, cursing his disobedient tongue.

"So that's why you're in such a good mood."

"It is not. I'm just happy."

"To have Nicole in your life."

"Nothing is going on between Nicole and me," Alex curtly denied. Though he couldn't deny that he wished there was.

"You spent the entire day with her and you enjoyed her company, didn't you?"

"Yes." Alex sighed resignedly. "I did, but…"

"But nothing," Victor interrupted and sat forward hopefully. "Are you seeing her tonight?"

"No." Alex gave his brother an exasperated look. "We're not dating, Vic."

"Yet," Victor predicted.

"What do you have planned for tonight?" Alex tried to divert him from the present topic of conversation.

"Nothing." Victor sighed dramatically and plopped back in his chair. "I'm all yours."

"What if I don't want you?" Alex drily asked.

"Too bad—you're stuck with me." Alex smiled as Victor's sandwich-filled hand halted midway to his mouth. "Hey, you wanna pop by Monique and Nicole's?"

Alex did, but he fought against it. "Nah. Nicole said they were heading out to a movie tonight."

"So you cared enough to check out her plans for to-night." Victor looked extremely pleased. "That doesn't sound like you were ready to be rid of her."

"No, I…"

"Yes, go on." Victor laughed at Alex's uneasy expression. "It's good to see you interested in a woman again."

"Vic, I'm not interested in Nicole." How he calmly told such a blatant lie, he'd never know.

"Save it, brother. We both know you like Nicole, and to my surprise, she likes you, too."

"Does she?" Alex grabbed Victor's beer and took a swig.

"You know she does," Victor confirmed. "Take a chance, bro. It's time for you to get back on the horse." He paused before threatening, "I don't want to interfere, but you know I will."

"Oh, no." Alex's smile turned into a frown. "You stay out of this."

"That depends on you, bro." Victor retrieved his beer. "That depends on you."

He laughed as Alex picked up a pillow from the sofa and threw it at him.

Nicole had been waiting for Monday morning to arrive so that she could see Alexander again. She was in the break room getting a cup of coffee when the door opened, admitting the man who had occupied her thoughts for the past thirty-six hours.

"Good morning," she greeted, willing her heart to stop thudding.

"Good morning," Alex said.

"Coffee?" At his nod, she poured him a cup.

"Thanks." He took the cup from her and sat down, then motioned for her to do the same. "Did you enjoy the rest of your weekend?"

"It was wonderfully relaxing." She sighed contentedly, sitting opposite him. "How about you?"

"It was great." He sipped his black coffee. "I did a little work and tried to keep Victor from eating me out of house and home." He chuckled at the memory.

"Do you two live together?"

"No. Well, not technically. He has his own place, but somehow it's just too much trouble for him to stock up on groceries, so he shows up at my house quite a bit."

"You wouldn't have it any other way," Nicole accused, and he grinned.

"Probably not." He leaned forward and whispered, "But don't tell him I said so."

"Your secret's safe with me."

"You look nice today." At Alexander's unexpected words, she nearly spilled her coffee. She glanced down at her kelly-green skirt suit and then back into his appreciative eyes.

"Thank you."

"After the staff meeting, I'd like to work with you on the ball gown sketch."

"All right." Nicole blinked as he changed directions on her again. Trying to keep up with him was challenging. "I've been giving it a lot of thought since we last talked about it."

"Good. I can't wait to see what you've come up with." He picked up his cup and stood. "See you later."

"Later," she echoed as he left.

Alone, she released her breath on a noisy sigh. Picking up her napkin, she fanned herself vigorously. That man was just too dangerously handsome for his own good—or hers. She pushed her nearly full coffee cup away, suddenly feeling the need to submerge her feverish body in a vat of ice water instead of sipping on the hot beverage before her.

* * *

The morning flew by, and before Nicole knew it, she was ensconced in Alexander's office with him working on the gown they were designing together for the upcoming fashion show. It was nerve-racking being alone with him in such close proximity. They sat side by side in front of massive windows on matching tall stools with easels, various pencils, watercolors and paint brushes at their disposal.

They had been working nonstop, and both had long since discarded their jackets. Nicole's sleeveless blouse left her arms bare, and Alex had rolled up the sleeves of his white shirt, exposing his hair-sprinkled, muscled forearms.

"What do you think?" Nicole held up the sketch for Alexander's review.

"Oh, yeah." He nodded approvingly. "That's coming together very nicely."

"I think so, too." Pleased with his praise, she placed the sketch back on the easel. "Thank you for this opportunity, Alexander."

"No thanks are necessary. You earned it. Your work is good—for a beginner."

Alex had teasingly called her a beginner but was rewarded when she smiled. She had the most beautiful smile.

When his eyes focused on her mouth in increasing intensity, her smile slowly faded and her lips parted slightly in anticipation and invitation. His eyes rose to lock on hers, and instead of moving away as common sense dictated, he placed a hand on her bare arm and lowered his head toward hers slowly, giving her sufficient time to pull away, which he soon realized she had no intention of doing.

"Hey, Alex, do you want to grab some lunch?" Victor breezed unannounced into the office. When he spotted Nicole sitting closely beside her brother, his smile widened. "Nicole, it's good to see you."

Victor ignored the silent warning in his brother's stormy gaze. He pulled Nicole off her stool and kissed both of her cheeks, then hugged her tight until she laughed.

"What are you doing here, Victor?" Alex cursed his brother's lousy timing—or perhaps it was fortuitous he had arrived and stopped him from making an unprofessional mistake.

"It's been too long, Nicole." Victor purposefully ignored Alex for the moment. "We'll have to do lunch soon."

"I'd love that." Nicole smiled. "Where have you been hiding?"

"Work has been crazy." He theatrically wiped his brow. "I've barely had time to bug Alex."

"If only." Alex's tone was dry, made more so by the fact that he was perturbed by his brother's interruption and his and Nicole's friendly manner. As if sensing his thoughts, Victor laughed, only incensing him further. "Victor, what do you want?"

"What's wrong with you, bro?"

"Nothing." Alex treated him to a pointed glance. "Except, as usual, you're interrupting my work."

"Oh, is that what you were doing when I came in?" Victor leaned on his desk. "It didn't look like you were working too hard."

"Victor…" Alex growled, glancing at Nicole's averted head. "I'm warning you."

Victor laughed and focused his attention on Nicole. "If I wasn't so self-confident, he'd give me an inferiority complex."

Nicole shook her head at him. "I don't think there's much chance of that."

"You know it," Victor agreed with a wink.

"Victor." Alex shot daggers at him. "I'm working now."

"I hope you're working on asking Nicole out to dinner,"

Victor blatantly suggested. "You seemed to be headed in the right direction when I entered."

"I swear one day I'm going to cut your tongue out," Alex threatened, to which Victor only chuckled.

"I'm just trying to help you out, bro."

"I don't need any help." What he needed was for him to get out of here.

"You could have fooled me," Victor mumbled loudly.

"Get outta here before I resort to violence." Alex took a few steps forward, and Victor retreated toward the door.

"Okay, I'm going." He held up his hands in surrender and promised Nicole, "I'll call you about lunch."

"Please do." She repressed a laugh and returned his wave as he hastily exited.

"I swear he wasn't raised in a barn," Alex vowed once they were alone again, and Nicole laughed at his obvious angst.

"I love seeing you two together," she confessed.

"Why?"

"Because your interactions are too cute."

"Cute?" Alex crossed his arms over his chest.

"Mmm-hmm." Nicole nodded. "He knows just the right buttons to push to get under your skin, and you pretend to be annoyed, but you're really not. You'd do anything for him, and he'd do the same for you."

"You've gleaned all that from our interactions?"

"Yes." She watched him closely. "Is my analysis wrong?"

No, she was right on target. Not only was she beautiful, she was also intuitive, unnerving and completely captivating. Damn, he loved being around her. Why did she have to be his employee, and why was it so easy for him to forget that as such, she was completely off-limits to him?

"I think we need to plunge the neckline a little lower." Instead of answering her, Alexander picked up a pencil and proceeded to modify their design. Nicole smiled and sat down beside him.

"Any lower, it will be at the navel," she joked.

"The word is *sexy,*" Alex informed and continued modifying the sketch. After a few minutes, he was satisfied with the results. "See? Sexy."

Nicole glanced at the Grecian-inspired gown and couldn't help but agree. "Extremely sexy."

"Mmm-hmm, very sexy." His eyes were focused on her instead of the gown, and she gulped at his blatantly hungry gaze. "What color do you think would be best?"

Nicole studied the sketch, tilted her head from side to side and chewed on her lower lip thoughtfully. Alex's eyes were drawn to her mouth, and he fought valiantly not to cover it with his own.

"To me it screams black and white," she finally decided. "More black than white, maybe just white highlights peeking out from the bottom of the skirt."

"Excellent choice." Alex reached back onto his desk and pulled out a sheet of fabric samples to show her. "See, we're completely in sync."

"Absolutely. We work well together."

"Yes, we do."

As she gazed into his warm, appreciative eyes, she wondered if that description would ever apply to them personally. She certainly hoped that it would.

Chapter 9

A little after 8:30 that night, Alexander left his office to go home when a movement in the corner of his eye distracted him. From across the partially illuminated room, half-hidden in shadows, Alexander watched Nicole at her desk as she stretched, and an elemental hunger raced through him. It was absurd how much he wanted to kiss her—and he didn't want to stop with a kiss. Conflicted eyes shifted to her moist, berry-colored lips that called to him without saying a word. *Oh, God!*

He feasted on every move she made, and when she set her pencil down, she stretched her arms in front of her and above her head before resting them behind her neck and arching back—a movement that accentuated her round breasts and shot primitive hunger through him.

She beckoned to him like a cold drink of water would to a thirsty man. There was no denying he was parched and had been for years. Not for casual female companionship; he had been at no shortage for that. He longed for something deeper, more lasting, something he feared Nicole could give him. If he let her.

He told himself to turn around and leave, but he didn't. Maybe it was the dim romantic lighting of the half-dark office; maybe it was the gnawing desire in the pit of his stomach that intensified daily. He didn't know, but his feet, with a will of their own, slowly approached Nicole's desk instead of turning and walking away as they should have. When he came to within a few feet, she jumped and swiveled around in his direction.

"It's just me," he said when he heard her gasp.

"Alexander." She placed a hand to her throat. "I don't care what you say, you enjoy startling me."

"I promise I don't." He leaned against her desk. He loved the way that she—unlike everyone else—used his entire first name instead of abbreviating it. "What are you doing here so late?"

Her hand gestured toward the piece of paper on her desk. "Working on this sketch."

"Pack it in until tomorrow," he ordered.

"You're still here," she softly accused.

"I'm the boss."

"I'm dedicated."

"Yes, I know you are, but you're not going to be any good to me if you work yourself into exhaustion."

"I won't. I just hate to stop now." She glanced regretfully at her sketch. "I'm almost finished."

"It'll be here tomorrow. Besides, you can't rush perfection."

"Well, I can't argue with that." She reached for her jacket and winced in discomfort.

Alex frowned. "What's wrong?"

"Nothing." She rubbed her aching shoulder with one hand. "Just stiff muscles. I've been working on this sketch for quite a while."

"Here." He walked behind her chair and pushed her hand aside. "Let me."

"Alexander…" Her voice trailed off as his strong fingers dug into her tired muscles.

"Hmm?"

"Um…" Her voice trailed off, and she closed her eyes.

"Yes?"

"Don't stop what you're doing," she softly ordered.

"I won't," he promised. "Now sit back."

She did as instructed, placing her jacket on her lap and all but melting as his talented fingers kneaded her tense shoulders and neck. His hands slid down her bare arms to her wrists and slowly back up again. Lord, her skin was soft and beckoned his fingers to touch her everywhere.

"You're tense." He concentrated on working out the kinks with difficulty. "I guess that's my fault for being so demanding."

"Don't be silly." She fought a moan, and he sensed that perhaps his fingers had created a different type of tension within her. "I love working here."

"Good." The flowery scent of her perfume wafted up to tease his nostrils. She smelled wonderful, and he'd bet she tasted even better.

"Mmm." She sighed as his thumbs circled the base of her neck. "Right there."

"There?" At her nod, his hands made their way under the sweetheart neckline of her blouse, and he slid his fingers up and down her neck and shoulders.

The touch of his flesh against hers almost sent him over the edge into madness, but he maintained his sanity somehow. However, when she purred deep in her throat and softly spoke his name on a serrated sigh of desire, that was his undoing.

Swiveling her chair, he pulled her up out of her seat until her soft body was pressed against his solid one, and without giving her or himself time to think, he fused his lips to hers. Her mouth was opened in a gasp of surprise, which he took full advantage of, slipping his seeking tongue past the barrier of her teeth in search for hers.

Oh, my Lord! Kissing her, thoroughly and properly, was even better than he had dreamed. Stopping wasn't an option. Tasting more of her incredible mouth was his only objective, and he carried out that mission with a vengeance.

Nicole's hands flexed at his solid shoulders before her arms snaked around his neck, entwining tightly. His hands moved to her back, fingers spread wide, trying to caress as much of her as possible, pressing her tight against the noticeable bulge in his groin, trailing up her sides, before finally moving to the back of her head, anchoring her mouth in place while their lips dueled for supremacy.

Alexander wanted to rip her blouse apart, followed by the rest of her clothes, needing to feel her naked flesh caressing his. The mere thought sent him into action; anxious fingers moved to her chest, unbuttoning one, two, three buttons and then slipping inside to slide across her warm inviting flesh, dipping purposefully into the valley between her breasts. Nicole shivered, which urged him on.

Needing to taste the flesh his fingers had uncovered, he reluctantly removed his mouth from hers to rest in the crook of her neck, white teeth biting at her softly scented flesh before trailing down to her collarbone. He placed feverish kisses along the tops of her breasts as they peeked out from her lacy bra.

He heard her moan invitingly, and her hands went behind his head, holding his mouth closer to her. The breathy moans and sighs she was making, and her complete capitulation, were all driving him wild. Unable to stand not kissing her, his mouth made the quick trip back up her neck until his lips settled against hers again. Amid a series of carnal kisses, he knew he was nearing the point of no return, but he didn't care. He wanted and needed her, and she wanted him too; that was the simple, complicated truth.

Nicole's hands burrowed underneath his shirt to touch his muscled chest. She smiled against his wonderfully bruising mouth when he groaned. As her hard nails scraped across his lightly hair-covered chest before moving low on his washboard abs, they moaned in unison. He was so warm and inviting; she longed to strip herself naked, snuggle against his bare flesh and never leave his arms again. She was lost in sensation, where nothing akin to right or wrong or reason existed—only passion, only pleasure.

Seeking fingers entwined in the hair at Alexander's nape, holding on for dear life as he destroyed her with one ravaging kiss after another. Her heart was thudding so fiercely, she thought it would break free from her chest— or was it his? She was quickly losing the capacity for rational thought, hedonistic, insane need replacing reason. All she wanted was for Alexander to keep kissing her and never let her go; she wanted to be absorbed by him. She wanted pleasure—pure, insane, lascivious pleasure—and she wanted it now!

Nicole felt like fainting but didn't dare. Instead, she pressed tighter against his inflexible strength. He moaned against her mouth in approval, sending delicious vibrations across her lips as their tongues turned from fierce competitors to suave seducers, sliding softly yet urgently together, trying to coax each to their will. Their hands moved feverishly over each other in an attempt to familiarize and savor their wonderful differences in tone, texture and girth.

There wasn't a doubt in Alex's mind that he would have taken her here and now, had not the sound of the cleaning cart being wheeled down the hall pulled him out of his lustful trance. Thankfully, as he half listened, the sound grew fainter, and he knew they were still alone in the room.

Good God, what was he doing carrying on like this, in the office of all places? He reluctantly, and with difficulty, coaxed his mouth from hers and rested his forehead against hers. They both breathed heavily while fighting to control the inferno still raging within them.

This was the kiss both had been longing for since their first teasing kiss in her hotel room, and it certainly hadn't disappointed. The only complaint she had was the fact that their embrace had ended it far too prematurely.

"I'm sorry, Nicole," he hoarsely offered when he could articulate again.

"Sorry?" She opened passion-glazed eyes to stare into his conflicted ones.

Removing her hands from his stomach, he held on to them tightly, wishing she would stop looking at him like that—as if he was all she wanted. Lord knew at this moment, all he wanted was her. He closed his eyes briefly to block out the entrancing sight of her.

This was a mistake. Getting involved with his employee was a mistake he wouldn't make again. The two of them together was wrong, but how could he escape the fact that when he was in her presence, nothing had ever felt so right?

"I shouldn't have done that." He spoke more for his benefit than hers—if only he believed what he said.

"But Alexander..."

He released her hands and stepped back. The sexy way she said his name was nearly his undoing.

"I'm sorry," he repeated before striding quickly away while he still could. He knew he should give her a ride home, but he didn't trust himself to be around her for another second without finishing what they had started.

* * *

Nicole watched, confused, as he quickly strode from the room, entered the elevator and never looked back. She sank down onto her chair and placed a trembling hand to her-still tingling mouth, while she pulled her gaping blouse closed. In the blink of an eye, everything had suddenly changed for her. Yes, Alexander was her boss, and no, she hadn't been seeking a romantic relationship with him; however, she could no longer deny the sizzling attraction between them, and she doubted that he would be able to either.

Bending down, she picked up her jacket, which had fallen to the floor when Alexander had pulled her into his arms. At the memory, she closed her eyes briefly, reliving the wonderful feel of his lips and body on hers. Until tonight, she hadn't known a kiss or caress could make her want so much—a realization she was certain Alexander shared.

Alexander. What was she going to do about him, about them? She ran her tongue over her lower lip. It tasted of him and their passion. Closing her eyes, she took several steadying breaths to try and calm the unfulfilled desire within her, but to no avail.

After the steamy kisses they had shared tonight, she knew without a doubt that something personal was brewing between them. Neither of them was going to be able to deny that any longer.

It would be complicated and perhaps a bit risky, but they could have something spectacular if Alexander would give them a chance—something she wanted very much.

Nicole made it home from the office a little after 9:00 p.m. For the entirety of the train ride, she had relived her and Alexander's kiss and his hasty retreat afterward.

"Nicole, is that you?" Monique's voice drifted from the kitchen.

"Yes." Nicole placed her purse and keys on the table. "It's me."

"Are you hungry? I made some pasta."

"That sounds great." She collapsed on the sofa. "I'll get some in a minute."

"Stay there. I'll bring you a plate," Monique offered.

"You're too good to me."

"I don't want you to move out." Monique winked as she exited the kitchen holding a plate of fettuccini Alfredo and a glass of white wine.

"There's absolutely no chance of that." Nicole took the glass and plate, placing them on the table in front of her. "Thanks."

"You're welcome." Monique sat beside her on the sofa. Her eyes widened as she intensely studied her.

"What?" Nicole shifted uncomfortably. "Do I have something on my face?"

"Um, no, but your lipstick is smudged."

"Is it?" Nicole cursed herself for not checking after Alexander's kiss. No wonder she had received several curious stares on the train.

"Mmm-hmm, very smudged."

"I was eating…"

"Alex?"

"Monique!" Nicole gasped, embarrassed by how accurate she was.

"Sorry." Monique didn't look at all sorry. "Who kissed you, Nicole?"

"No one." She took a bite of pasta. "This is delicious."

"Thanks, but no changing the subject. Come on—out with it."

"All right." Nicole sighed, sipped her wine and admitted, "Alexander kissed me."

"So you were eating…"

"Monique." At Nicole's stern interruption, her friend laughed.

"I knew you two liked each other."

"I do like him," Nicole admitted, taking another drink of her wine. "But he is still my boss, and I don't want people inferring he hired me for anything other than my artistic talents."

"Honey, people will always find a reason to talk about you," Monique wisely informed. "My advice is to not worry about what other people think."

"Maybe you're right." Nicole was silent while she ate several forkfuls of fettuccini. "I am in Paris now. Maybe I should go with the flow and see what develops with Alexander."

"Well, finally!" Monique laughingly approved. "That must have been some kiss to make you do a complete turnaround."

"It was." Nicole's eyes grew dreamy at the memory. "Or rather, they were."

"Vive la romance!" Monique proclaimed, and Nicole raised her glass in silent salute.

Chapter 10

The next day, as Nicole had expected and anticipated, Alexander called her into his office as soon as she sat down at her desk. She took a few minutes to lock up her purse before going to Alexander's office. She paused at his closed door, smoothed her palms over the front of her turquoise and black dress, took a deep breath and knocked.

"Come in," Alexander's voice beckoned, and she opened the door, then closed it softly behind her.

"Good morning, Alexander." She walked toward his desk.

"Good morning." He looked stern and didn't return her smile. "We need to talk about last night."

"I know." She sat down in the chair in front of his desk.

He resumed his seat behind the desk, thinking it wise to have some space between them. They stared at each other silently, each waiting for the other to begin.

"You're a very beautiful woman, Nicole." He leaned forward, placing his palms on his desk. "It goes without saying that any man would be attracted to you, and I'm no exception."

"Thank you for the compliment."

"It's the truth." He didn't sound happy about that fact. They eyed each other silently before he sighed heavily and came to his main point. "I'm your boss and you're my employee, and as such, I can't and won't allow anything untoward to develop between us—regardless of the fact that we're obviously attracted to each other."

"I completely agree, Alexander."

"You do?" Surprise flickered in his eyes.

"Of course." She crossed her legs. "We simply got carried away last night. I know I'm here to work and learn and not engage in an office romance—" She paused before saying, "Especially not with you."

"Why not with me?"

"Because, as you correctly stated, you're my boss," she softly reminded him.

"Right." He curtly nodded.

She was right, and he was right. So why was her immediate and complete agreement so distasteful? She smiled as if she didn't have a care in the world, and it angered him. Why was she happy about him basically brushing her off?

"I don't want there to be any awkwardness between us," she continued.

"Neither do I." He stood and extended his hand. "Still friends?"

"Of course." She stood and shook his hand. He held her hand a little longer than necessary, reluctant to release her. "Is there anything else?"

"No." He finally dropped her hand. "You can get back to work."

"I'll have that design for you by lunchtime," she promised.

"Good."

He turned his chair to glance out the window, and when he glanced back she was gone.

His frown intensified as he contemplated their remarkably civil meeting. She seemed okay with what he had said, and she herself had said all the right things; however, he hoped she wasn't happy about them maintaining only a business relationship because Lord knew he wasn't. No matter how ill-advised it was, he wanted her badly, and ego wouldn't allow him to believe she didn't want him just as much.

But they couldn't act upon that attraction. His frown deepened.

Or could they?

When Nicole made it back to her desk, the phone was ringing. She snatched up the receiver and perched on the edge of her desk.

"Nicole Carter."

"Hey, gorgeous. It's Victor."

"Hi, Victor. What's up?"

"I'm hoping you're free for lunch today."

"With you? Anytime."

"Now, that's what I like to hear." She heard the smile in his voice. "Pick you up around one?"

"Perfect. See you then."

"Great. Bye."

"Bye, Victor." She rang off, sat down and began to work.

The morning flew by, and promptly at one o'clock, Nicole glanced up from her sketch just as Victor exited the elevator. Alexander, who happened to be out in the design area, smiled when his brother approached, patted him on the back and said a few words in greeting before Victor continued toward Nicole's desk. Alexander's smile turned into a frown as he watched Victor take Nicole's hand, help her out of her chair and kiss her cheeks before placing a friendly arm around her shoulders as they walked toward the elevator.

"Going somewhere?" Alex pointedly glanced at Nicole.

"Yep." Victor smiled and answered for her. "I'm stealing Nicole away for lunch."

"Oh." That single word carried a multitude of emotion. "I didn't realize you came to see Nicole."

"When I come to see you, I'm always accused of interrupting your work," Victor reminded him.

"You usually are." Though he spoke to his brother, his eyes were glued on Nicole, who remained silent but treated him to an innocent smile.

"Well, not this time." Victor pulled Nicole closer, and Alex's eyes narrowed. "Wanna join us?"

"No, thanks." His tightly worded refusal made her think he didn't want her to leave the office, but that was ridiculous.

"Okay, your loss." Victor waved, pulled Nicole into the elevator and deliberately bent down to whisper in her ear, "Can I convince you to be a bum with me for the rest of the day?"

"You can try." She laughed.

The smile on Nicole's face slowly fell when she glanced up and found Alexander staring intensely at them until the doors closed.

Once outside, Victor and Nicole walked a short distance to the corner café. They sat outside under a green-and-white-striped umbrella.

"Alex is a goner," Victor predicted. "He didn't appreciate me taking you to lunch." He rubbed his hands together gleefully. "He was so jealous, he couldn't see straight."

"No, he wasn't." Her eyes widened as she stared at Victor's grinning countenance. "Was he?"

"You bet he was." He chuckled before laughing heartily.

Nicole was appalled. She knew he had seemed upset, but she had thought it was because of their talk earlier. Was he really jealous of Victor? Oh, God, she hoped not.

"Victor, this is not funny."

"You're right—it's fabulous," he corrected. "He's finally coming to terms with his feelings for you. Are you?"

"Am I what?"

"You know what," he admonished. "Are you coming to terms with your feelings for him?" At her pregnant silence he challenged, "Tell me you're not attracted to him."

"Maybe he's not attracted to me," she countered, and Victor laughed heartily again.

"That's one thing you don't have to worry about." He sipped his drink. "He's plenty attracted to you."

"I'm here to work, Victor." Though his assertion thrilled her, she thought it best not to discuss Alexander with him.

"I swear." He sighed loudly. "I have enough trouble trying to get Alex to loosen up. Don't tell me I'm going to have to work on you, too."

"Why are you so intent on us getting together?"

"Because I want him to be happy, and when he met you, a flame that had been long dormant in him sparked to life. You're the first woman he's been interested in since—" He stopped himself from revealing too much.

"Since Nina Laurent?" she softly asked.

His eyes widened. "What do you know about Nina the barracuda?"

"Nothing really." Nicole chuckled at his unflattering description. "Crystal mentioned her when I asked her why she dislikes me."

"That—" he paused, searching for a word "—witch! I'll—"

"No, you won't." Nicole touched his clenched fist. "I don't need you, Monique or anyone else to fight my battles."

"No, you don't. You're tough," he said. "I really can't talk about Nina. That's Alex's albatross."

"That's okay. It's none of my business." She might not know the specifics, but she could put two and two together and come up with four. "Don't tell Alexander I mentioned her."

"I won't, but I am going to keep pushing you two together," he promised, laughing when she shook her head at him.

From the cash register across the room, Alexander watched his brother and Nicole engaged in cozy conversation. It was just his luck that they had all chosen the same café for lunch. He switched his order to carryout as he glared at the couple sitting under the umbrella outside.

He nearly blew a gasket when Nicole covered Victor's hand with hers, and he brought her hand to his lips, eliciting a laugh from her. When had they become so chummy? What was she doing kissing him one night and cozying up to his brother the next day? What type of game was she playing?

Women! They weren't to be trusted. If he had begun to forget that, Nicole's behavior brought that truism back into crystal clear focus for him.

He paid for his lunch, snatched his bag off the counter and stalked out without being seen by the cozy couple who seemed to only have eyes for each other.

After a wonderful lunch, Nicole returned to the office promptly at two o'clock. She had resisted Victor's urging to stay a little longer, not wanting to take advantage by extending her lunch break beyond the usual hour. She had no sooner disembarked from the elevator than Alexander stormed out of his office.

"I need to see you. Now," he frostily ordered and then turned and walked back to his office.

Frowning, Nicole followed his rapidly retreating back. He stood woodenly in front of his desk as she entered.

"Shut the door," he stiffly ordered.

She complied, then walked over until she was standing a few feet away from him. "What is it?"

"What took you so long at lunch?"

"Long?" An arched eyebrow rose at his accusatory tone. "I was only gone an hour."

He glanced at his watch. "It seemed longer."

"What's wrong, Alexander?"

I saw you cozying up to my brother at lunch—that's what's wrong, he wanted to answer. Of course, he said no such thing.

"Nothing." He turned his back on her. "I wanted to discuss something with you, that's all."

She walked to his side and touched his taut arm. "What?"

"It doesn't matter now." Turning, he covered her hand to remove it from his arm, but she entwined her fingers with his instead.

"Alexander." She moved closer to him. "Victor and I are just friends."

"You don't owe me an explanation."

"Obviously I do, since you're so jealous you can't see straight."

"Jealous?" He balked at her correct observation. "Don't flatter yourself."

"You flatter me," she softly returned.

"I am not jealous, Nicole." At her disbelieving look, he reminded her, "Just this morning, we both agreed there can be nothing between us. You're free to date whomever you please." But the thought of her with anyone else was eating him alive, no matter how he tried to deny it.

"Do you want me to date Victor?"

"No," he answered honestly without thinking. At her knowing smile, he added, "It doesn't matter to me one way or the other."

"The thought of me kissing another man doesn't bother you?"

"Why should it?" Who did he think he was kidding?

"Alexander." She placed her hands on his rigid shoulders. "After last night, do you really think I want anyone else?" She felt emboldened by Victor's lunchtime observations that Alexander wanted her, by their fiery kisses last night and by Alexander's obvious angst at the possibility of her dating someone else.

"Nicole, we both agreed—"

"I know what we agreed." She moved closer to him still. "Tell me you want to see me with someone else, and this conversation is over," she promised.

They stared at each other for an intense second before his arms went around her waist and hauled her against him. He held her close for a few seconds before his hands released her waist to frame her face, fingers tracing every beautiful curve while his eyes watched, fascinated. His thumb undertook an exquisitely thorough exploration of her lower lip before his hands exerted slight pressure, tilting her head back while he stared deeply into her inviting eyes.

Oh, Alexander, she thought. *I know this is complicated. I understand you've been hurt, but give me a chance—give us a chance.* She wondered if he could read the silent invitation written in her eyes.

She smiled in triumph when, after an eternity, his mouth

lowered toward hers, proof that her message had been received. She met him halfway and he treated her mouth to butterfly kisses, torturing them both. His teeth nipped at her lower lip before his tongue had its way. She sighed raggedly as his mouth played a seductive game of cat and mouse with hers. Finally, unable to bear it another second, her arms encircled his neck, hands resting on the back of his head, fusing his mouth to hers.

His mouth rested against hers, their warm breath intermingling as he coaxed her lips apart. He sent his tongue in strategic search of hers. Once finding its target, they engaged in a frenzied competition of hide and seek. They tilted their heads one way then another, using different angles to taste more of each other, and still it wasn't enough to satisfy either of them.

His hands moved to the back zip of her dress, sliding it downward, allowing his hands to work the garment off her shoulders. He investigated the satiny flesh exposed by his wayward hands, and after feasting on her delectable mouth for long seconds, his lips blazed a trail of fire down her jaw to her throat before traversing her shoulders and collarbone. Nicole gasped as pure pleasure splintered throughout her at Alexander's expert caresses.

"Alexander." She moaned his name.

He bit the fleshy part of her breast visible from the top of her bra hard enough to cause a gasp from her and to leave a mark. He wanted and needed to brand her as his. His rough tongue licked across the spot several times before her hands framed his face, pulling his head away from her chest and bringing his mouth back to hers. Pure, destructive, white-hot passion erupted between them.

His hands moved to her waist, lifting her so that she was sitting on the edge of his desk. Hands on her inner thighs spread her legs wide, and he positioned himself between them. He kissed her erotically and growled against her delicious lips when she hooked a leg around his waist and pulled his lower body into closer, more intimate contact with hers. His hands sought out her bare back while he slowly lowered her to the desktop.

He didn't know whether to thank or curse the shrill ringing of the phone, which snapped him back from the brink of insanity just in the nick of time. The instrument rang a few more annoying times before silencing, but it had achieved the same effect as a douse of cold water. Alexander pulled them upright, tore his mouth from hers and took a step away from temptation.

"Fix your dress," he ordered tersely, and she pulled the garment back on her shoulders, stood and presented her naked back to him so that he could zip her up. "You can use my bathroom to repair your lipstick." *And give me some time to regain some semblance of control.*

He pointed to a door to the right of his desk. Without a word, she walked into his bathroom and made sure she was presentable to her fellow coworkers. When she returned, he was standing gazing out of the window with his back to her.

"You'd better get back to work," he suggested without turning around.

"Yes, you're right." She started toward the door but stopped and turned around again. "Alexander?"

He sighed heavily before turning to glance at her—his beautiful Nicole. *His? What the…?* Oh, boy! Even as he berated himself, he knew there was no denying it; that was exactly the way he thought of her—as *his. Damn!*

They worked together. They shouldn't start anything—but could they stop it? Could he ignore his powerful unexpected feelings for her? Did he even want to try?

"Alexander?" She called his name again, rousing him out of his contemplative state.

"Yes?"

"I know neither of us expected this."

"No," he agreed. *That was an understatement if he ever heard one.*

"I'm very attracted you—" she paused and confidently added "—and you feel the same way about me." At his silent agreement she concluded, "I don't think we're going to be able to contain this passion between us much longer."

Without waiting for his response—which was good because he didn't have a satisfactory one—she turned and exited, leaving him to ponder her wise words and his alarming feelings.

Chapter 11

Alexander wasn't in the next day. Nicole wondered if he was trying to avoid her but quickly dismissed that. He wouldn't boycott his own company because of the sexual tension between them. She deliberately walked past his open office door several times, and on her third pass found Victor standing behind Alexander's desk poking in drawers.

"Hi, Victor." Nicole stuck her head through the doorway and walked fully into the office when he waved her inside. "What's going on?"

"Hey, Nicole." He glanced up from stuffing a bag with Alexander's belongings. "How are you?"

"I'm fine. Where's Alexander?"

"At home, sick."

"Sick? He was fine last night."

"Please don't mention last night." Victor groaned. "I'm trying to forget it ever happened."

"What happened?"

"I borrowed Alex's beloved Ferrari, and I offered to drive him home, but he said he'd take a cab and ended up in a fender bender."

"Oh, my God!" Nicole placed a hand to her heart. "Are you sure he's okay?"

"He's fine. He just aggravated an old back injury. His doctor told him to stay home for a few days."

Nicole glanced at him skeptically. "Alexander listened to him?"

"Nope." Victor chuckled at the memory. "I threatened to come to work with him and follow him around all day if he came in."

"That would do it." Nicole laughed.

"That was the idea." He winked and then sighed. "He's such a baby when he's sick."

A skeptical eyebrow rose. "And you're not?"

"Of course not." At her doubtful glance he added, "You know I'm always a joy to be around."

"And I also know that all men turn into big babies when they're sick," Nicole teased.

"We just hate feeling helpless."

"Mmm-hmm."

"I'm gonna leave that subject alone," Victor wisely decided. "Why don't you quit a little early today and drop by the house to see him?"

"I don't think I should, Victor." She wanted to, but wasn't sure how Alexander would react if she did. "We're so busy now. I'm sure Alexander wouldn't approve of me leaving early."

"Hey, I'm part owner and I say you should and can." His stern order made her smile. "Besides, he'd love to see you, and it would be a *big* favor to me."

"To you? How?"

"He's driving me crazy." Victor made a choking imitation with his hands, and she laughed. "You can laugh,

but poor me! The guy can hire a nurse or anyone else he
needs, but he has to have me wait on him hand and foot,
like I don't have a business of my own to run."

"Maybe it makes him feel better having you around."

"Oh, no, that's not it," Victor denied, laughing. "He's
punishing me for *causing* his accident—as if I was driving the cab. Forget the fact that I offered to take him home.
He's so illogical."

"You two are such siblings."

"I know." Victor sighed dramatically and then glanced
at her hopefully. "So will you stop by?"

"Sure, and I'll even bring him dinner."

"Thank you, thank you!" Victor kissed her cheek and
hugged her tightly. "An hour or two off, oh, thank you!"

"You're welcome." Nicole laughed. "You're a nut."

"A tired nut." He sighed, releasing her. "You don't know
how demanding my brother can be."

"Say what?" She placed her hands on her hips, and he
laughed heartily.

"Sorry, I forgot you work with him." He gave her an understanding one-arm hug. "I won't tell him you're coming
by tonight. The surprise will do him good."

"Okay. I'll be there around six."

"Perfect. Do you know where his house is? Do you want
me to pick you up?"

"Yes, I know where he lives. I'll take a cab."

"Are you sure that's not too much trouble?"

"No, it'll be fine." At his skeptical look she continued, "I insist. Besides, you need your few hours'
rest." At her laughing reminder, he nodded vigorously
in agreement.

"I'll leave the key under the mat for you." He picked
up his laden bag and sighed. "Back to do my penance.
See you later."

"Bye, Victor." She waved him off.

* * *

Nicole left work around five, stopping to buy some groceries before heading to Alexander's house. She arrived a little after six and let herself in with the key Victor had left for her under the mat. She glanced around expectantly when the hall light flipped on, but she was alone in the huge foyer. It was quiet, and she was just about to announce herself when Alexander beat her to it.

"Victor, is that you?" Alexander's voice bellowed from the bedroom. "Where have you been? I'm hungry! Victor?"

Nicole smiled, walked toward his angry voice and opened the door to what she realized was his bedroom. The room was huge, making his king-size bed with polished hardwood headboard seem small. His bed was set up on a platform, and he looked like royalty lying there looking down on whoever entered his private domain. Matching mahogany hardwood cabinets took up one entire wall, and gleaming hardwood floors were the finishing touch to the gorgeously decorated room.

Alexander lay on the bed, bare-chested, covers over his lower body. She naughtily wondered if he was as naked below the covers as he was on top. Fine hairs sprinkled his muscular chest.

"Hi." She smiled, setting the groceries down in a chair and removing her purple jacket. She noted his eyes rake over her in appreciation. She was dressed in a sleeveless white dress covered in purple and lilac flowers.

"Nicole!" He pulled the covers up to his chest, and her smile widened. "What are you doing here?"

"I came to see how you are." She walked toward his bed.

"My no-good brother deserted me." His hands fisted at his sides. "This is all Victor's fault."

"He didn't desert you, Alexander." She fought a laugh at his dejected countenance. "I told him I'd stop by and check on you after work."

His eyes grew stormy. "Don't tell me he asked you to do that."

"It's not a problem," she quickly assured him. "When he stopped by to get your work things, we talked and he told me you were sick."

"Yeah, sick because of him."

"Oh, Alexander." She fought against running her fingers down his furrowed brow. "He feels really bad about your accident."

"He should," he quickly agreed, glancing at the bags in the chair by the door. "What's that?"

"Dinner."

"You don't have to cook me dinner, Nicole."

"I know I don't *have* to. I want to." She walked closer. "How are you feeling?"

"Stir-crazy, put-upon, fed up." He paused and frowned. "Will those adjectives do?" Her laughter coaxed a tiny smile out of him.

"Those will do just fine." She returned to the door and picked up the groceries again. "Let me get dinner going, and we'll see what we can do to improve your mood."

"What do you have in mind?"

"You'll see," she mysteriously replied. "Where's the kitchen?"

"Go back out to the foyer and take the hall to the left, keep straight, then make a right at the end of that hall. Follow the circle, and you'll be there." As she digested his directions, he started to get up. "It'll probably be better if I show you."

"Stay where you are. I can find it." Her stern voice kept him in bed. "Do you need anything?"

"No, I'm good."

"Okay, be back in a flash."

She left to prepare dinner. When she returned thirty

minutes later he had put on a white T-shirt and black pajama bottoms and lay on top of the white down comforter.

"Alexander, did you get out of that bed?"

"Yes." At her accusatory stare, he defended himself. "I can get up. My doctor just said do it as little as possible."

"Mmm-hmm." She placed a tray on his lap. "Maybe food will make you feel better."

"It smells and looks delicious. You went to too much trouble."

"It was no trouble. I love to cook, and this is a quick but filling recipe. I hope you like shrimp."

"Does a hog like slop?"

"I'll take that as a yes."

"You could have brought takeout." He ravenously eyed the plateful of shrimp scampi pasta, tossed salad on the side and fresh fruit for dessert.

"My mother would fly to Paris and scold me beyond reason if I dared bring someone who wasn't feeling well anything other than homemade food." She rolled her eyes heavenward, and he laughed. "I'll be right back." She left and returned a few minutes later with her own dinner tray and placed it on a bedside table. "And for entertainment." She took her notebook out of her bag.

"What are we watching?" He used the remote to switch on the TV, and she walked over and hooked up her notebook.

"You'll see." She smiled and sat down in the chair beside his bed with her dinner tray on her lap.

Soon the sounds of *I Love Lucy* filled the air. He stared at her with a big grin, and they both laughed.

"Great food, beautiful company and *Lucy.*" He smiled happily. "What more could a man want?"

"If *Lucy* can't lighten your mood, nothing can."

"You're doing a bang-up job all by yourself." The look he gave her stole her breath away.

"Eat up while it's hot," she ordered, and he picked up his fork, twirling spaghetti and spearing a plump piece of shrimp.

"Oh, God, this is delicious."

"Thank you." She picked up her own fork.

"That lousy brother of mine has been feeding me nothing but takeout." He dug into his meal with gusto. "Meal after meal of lousy takeout."

"Alexander, you've only been in bed since last night."

"Well it seems longer," he complained. "Especially since I haven't had a decent meal since yesterday, thanks to Victor."

"You leave poor Victor alone."

"Poor Victor?" He scowled. "Do you know what he did to me?"

"Yes, I heard, but Alexander, you know your accident really wasn't his fault."

"If he'd stop being cheap and buy his own Ferrari, this never would have happened," he grumbled, refusing to give his brother a break. "It's not like he can't afford it."

"Alexander." She tsked her tongue at him. "Be fair."

"All right. I know it was a freak accident," he slowly agreed around a smile. "But I have to give him a hard time, or I'll lose my big-brother card."

"We can't have that," she teased.

The episode started, and their eyes were glued to the set. They laughed, recited lines and made bets on who remembered the episode better. It soon became apparent that neither had been joking when they said they were die-hard fans. They made it through two episodes when Nicole took their clean plates into the kitchen. When she returned, they settled in to watch more *Lucy.*

"How long can you stay?" Alex asked when she removed her shoes and curled up in the plush chair beside his bed.

"As long as you want me to," she automatically promised.

* * *

Alexander's heart soared at her words. What was it about Nicole that he found so appealing? Why did he want to take hold of her and never let go?

"Good," he finally responded, and her soft smile informed him she somehow knew what he had been thinking.

The phone rang, and Alexander automatically reached for it without thinking and cursed under his breath when pain shot through his lower back. Damn, he hated being helpless!

"Are you okay?" At his nod Nicole picked up the phone and handed it to him. "Here you go."

"Thanks." He took the phone and answered. He listened before responding, "Yes, Nicole is here. Good thing, too, since my own brother deserted me."

"Alexander, be nice," Nicole whispered, and he winked at her.

"No, you don't need to come back tonight. I'm fine. Nicole made me a real dinner. Yeah, I know takeout was safer than your cooking." He laughed. "I've gotta go. We're watching television." He paused and then added drily, "Yes, Victor, that's all we're doing." Nicole blushed, and Alex shrugged apologetically. "What do you expect me to do with a hurt back? I'm hanging up now." He listened, chuckled and then said, "Yeah. I'll deal with you tomorrow—and take care of my baby, or I'll take care of you when I'm up and about. Okay, bye." He rang off and handed the phone back to Nicole. "Sorry about that."

"It's okay." She replaced the phone in its cradle. "Your brother is…"

"Something else," he finished, and she agreed with a nod.

"And then some."

"He's always been this way—bad to the bone," Alex said.

"He's not bad—just mischievous," Nicole corrected.

"You can say that again."

"I'm sure you spoiled him rotten growing up—and probably still do," she guessed. "So you can't blame him for expecting you always will."

"I suppose."

"I thought so," she responded after seeing his guilty smile. "Now, you leave Victor alone."

He liked the way she took up for Victor, which was something he had done his entire life—especially when his parents' marriage had started to fail many years before their deaths. They had metamorphosed from two loving parents into two strangers he and Victor couldn't stand to be around for more than five minutes; thus, he had moved out when he was nineteen and had fought tooth and nail to convince his parents to let him take Victor with him. They had given in eventually, and he had literally become Victor's parents in addition to being his brother.

She touched his arm. "Is anything wrong, Alexander?"

"No." He shook his head. "Let's get back to *Lucy*."

"Sounds good to me."

Though she agreed, he could feel her curiosity. He knew she had questions, and he appreciated her restraint in giving him his space by not asking a single one. He didn't want to talk about his parents—he had put too much time into trying to forget.

They were on the ninth episode when Nicole yawned, prompting Alex to glance at the bedside clock. It was late; the hours had flown by in Nicole's great company.

"Excuse me," she said. "What time is it?"

He glanced at the bedside clock. "A little after eleven."

"Is it that late?" She sat up, surprised, and slipped her shoes back on. "I'd better go."

"No." He grabbed her hand as she stood. "Stay the night." It was scary how much he wanted her to stay—right here, in his room, in his bed with him all night long.

"Alexander…?" Her heart somersaulted in her chest. She wanted to stay with him more than anything.

"I mean, it's too late for you to go home. I'd worry about you. You can stay in my guest room down the hall." He could have offered her one of the upstairs guest rooms, but he wanted her close by. He refused to ponder why.

"Well…" She seemed to consider it.

"Stay," he repeated.

"Okay."

"Good." He reluctantly released her hand. "Grab one of my shirts out of the drawer to sleep in."

"Thanks." She walked over and selected a red T-shirt. "Do you need anything before I turn in?"

"No, I'm good." That was a lie. He needed her. What he wouldn't give to have her curl up beside him.

"I'll see you in the morning," Nicole said. She didn't want to leave him and sensed he didn't want her to go either.

"Good night, Nicole," he finally said to alleviate the silence between them.

"Good night."

She left and made her way to the guest room, which was half the size of Alexander's but still extremely roomy. Plopping down onto the baby-soft quilt, she picked up the phone to call Monique and let her know she'd be staying at Alexander's. As expected, she had to endure some good-natured teasing from her roomie before ringing off. Then she took a hot shower and crawled into her blissfully comfortable bed, wearing Alexander's too-big T-shirt and trying to forget he was just down the hall, just out of reach.

Alex woke at 6:30 a.m., later than usual, to bright sunshine filtering through the window. He gingerly sat up and thankfully had only minimal pain. Sighing, he slowly got out of bed. A hot soak in the tub, and he'd be good to go. He didn't care what the doctor said; he was going into work today, but first his bath, and then he was going to cook breakfast for Nicole—his angel of mercy.

A smile lifted the corners of his mouth at the thought of her. She was a breath of fresh air—genuine, talented and caring. She was special, she made him feel alive again and he was dangerously close to forgetting—and even closer to breaking—his number-one rule, which was no romantic entanglements with his employees.

After his disastrous relationship with Nina Laurent— which had nothing to do with love and everything to do with necessity—it was a well-founded rule he hadn't been tempted to break until now, until meeting Nicole. It was funny and scary how much Nicole had changed his life for the better in such a short time. Scarier still was how hard it was to imagine his life without her in it.

An hour later, with breakfast tray in hand, Alexander made his way to his guest room where Nicole had slept. He hadn't heard any signs of her stirring yet and wondered if she was still sleeping.

Nicole?" He knocked on her door lightly. "Nicole?" He opened the door with one hand and peeped inside. She was still asleep.

He started to leave but unable to help himself, he walked into the room instead and placed the tray of French toast, scrambled eggs and juice on the dresser. Staring down at her, a strange feeling came over him—one of utter contentment. He liked having her in his house and would like it even more if she was sleeping in his bed. Man, he was losing all objectivity when it came to her, and he had no earthly idea of how to get it back.

The covers were pushed down to her waist, giving his greedy eyes an unobstructed view. She was lying on her back, one arm strewn restlessly over her head, the other lying across her stomach. She looked so peaceful, beautiful and desirable.

Unable to stop himself, he sat on the edge of the bed and smoothed her bangs away from her closed eyes. She stretched and turned over until her face trapped his hand under her cheek. He smiled and used his other hand to trace light patterns on her other cheek. She sighed, and her hand moved up to cover his. After a few seconds she slowly opened her eyes.

"Alexander?"

"The one and only." Her sleepy eyes became alert, and she rolled onto her back, releasing his hand.

"What are you doing out of bed?"

"I've been up for a while." He motioned to the tray on the dresser. "I even cooked you breakfast."

"Alexander, you didn't!" She sat upright. "You're supposed to be resting."

"I feel ninety percent better."

"Why don't you try for one hundred?"

"No can do. I've got too much work waiting for me at the office."

"You need to rest—"

He held up a hand, forestalling her words. "Nicole, I'm fine. I'm not one to sit around for too long. One day is about my maximum, unless I'm unconscious."

"Stubborn man."

"I am," he proudly agreed, and humor lit up her face.

"What time is it?"

"7:30."

"What?" Her eyes widened in shock. "I'm going to be late for work. I need to go home and change and—"

"Nicole, relax." His smile alleviated her angst. "Don't worry. I'm the boss," he reminded her.

"That's right. You are." She settled back against the pillows. "How do you feel, really?"

"Much better after your TLC." He stared deeply into her warm brown eyes and felt completely lost yet strangely found. "Thank you."

"You're welcome." After a slight hesitation, she sat up and placed a hand on his cheek. "That was a very nice thank you, but this is how you thank me properly." She boldly pulled his lips to hers.

He didn't even consider resisting her, but instead jumped headlong into the vortex of their desire. His mouth demanded capitulation from hers, and his seeking tongue stroked her lips and teeth before slipping inside of the warm recesses of her mouth, expertly stoking the fires of their passion.

They kissed madly—each holding nothing back. His hands found a way under her shirt to touch her bare back before running up her sides and inching toward her round breasts. She groaned against his bruising lips, threading her fingers into his hair, pulling his mouth tighter against hers as they ate voraciously from each other.

Each knew how this embrace would end, and they both welcomed the inevitable conclusion they had been skirting around for weeks. Nicole slowly reclined back onto the bed, drawing Alexander with her. When he winced against her mouth, she sat upright, forcing him to do the same.

"Your back!" She carefully pulled out of his arms. "I'm so sorry."

"No, it's all right."

"Are you sure you're okay?"

"I'm fine." He sat up slowly until completely erect and then stood. "I'd better let you eat your breakfast and get dressed."

"Let me help you back to your room." She threw back the covers and got out of bed.

His eyes dilated at how little his T-shirt covered, stopping right above midthigh. Damn, she had a body to die for, and he ached to explore every delectable inch of it. Mercy, he ached for this woman!

"No, I can manage." He backed away from her as if she was a dangerous predator.

"Are you sure?"

"Yes." He walked slowly to the door and turned to smile at her briefly before leaving.

Nicole sank onto the bed and sighed heavily, fingers touching her still-tingling lips, eyes sliding closed. She had it bad for that man. She couldn't stop her heart from fluttering when he entered a room or when he looked at her with those unique, expressive eyes of his. The sound of his voice was like a velvet caress on her skin, and she constantly craved the touch of his body and his lips since first tasting those forbidden fruits. She feared she always would.

Opening dreamy eyes, she came to a long overdue decision; she was through trying to rationalize and certainly through denying it—she wouldn't be satisfied until she had received everything from Alexander, until she had given him everything.

Chapter 12

Time flew by in a blur as they worked furiously getting ready for the fashion show that was in a little over a week. Neither Nicole nor Alexander made mention of the near consummation of their relationship at his house, and Nicole gave him the space he appeared to need. She knew he wouldn't be able to ignore their mutual desire much longer, and she could wait until he worked out his personal demons because she knew in her heart where they were headed and prayed they would reach their destination sooner rather than later.

It was April 21, Nicole's birthday, the first she would spend without her family. She hadn't allowed herself to think about that until receiving calls from her parents, brother and sister at work. In the afternoon, four huge, gaily colored bouquets of flowers arrived at work from home, bringing tears to her eyes.

"Hey, who sent the flower garden?" Monique eyed the

arrangements littering Nicole's desk and smiled teasingly. "The boss?"

"No." Nicole shook her head. "My family."

"What's the occasion?"

"It's my birthday today."

"What?" Monique's mouth fell open in shock. "Why didn't you tell me?"

"Honestly, we've been so busy, it slipped my mind."

"You're too young to want to forget your birthday," Monique accused. "How old are you?"

"Twenty-six." Nicole laughed.

"Three years younger than me. We need to celebrate tonight."

"That would be great, but by the time we get off, all I'm going to want to do is crash."

"Nicole, you can't spend your birthday working." Monique stared at her, aghast.

"Why not?"

"Because you can't!"

"There's no law against working on your birthday."

Monique placed a hand on her hip. "Well, there should be."

"It's just another day."

"Nicole, you have to…" Monique stopped and grabbed her stomach, and Nicole stood and touched her arm.

"Monique, what's wrong?"

"Oh, nothing. I just got a little pain in my stomach." At Nicole's worried glance she assured her. "I'll be fine. It's probably my lunch not agreeing with me. I've got some antacids in my office."

Nicole watched worriedly as her friend walked slowly back into her office. For the next hour, she kept a watchful eye on Monique, who stayed in her office and made phone calls with one hand pressed either to her stomach or her head. When she exited her office an hour later with her purse slung over her shoulder, Nicole wasn't a bit surprised.

"I think I might have gotten food poisoning, and the boss is letting me go home."

"Can you make it alone?" Nicole stood and walked her to the elevator.

"Yes. My cast-iron stomach will rebound in no time."

"I don't know, Monique…"

"I'll be okay. A little rest, and I'll be good as new." She squeezed her hand. "I promise I'll call my doctor if I don't feel any better. Besides, you'll be home in several hours."

"Still…"

"I'll be fine," Monique reiterated. "We'll celebrate your birthday when I'm feeling better."

"Don't worry about that," Nicole said dismissively. "Just feel better."

"I will." She entered the elevator. "See you tonight."

"Call me if you need anything, promise?"

"Promise."

For the past couple of hours, Nicole had kept watch on Monique by phone. Her roommate sounded much better and vowed she'd be at work tomorrow no matter what. Feeling relieved, Nicole threw herself into work, trying to forget she had no plans to celebrate her birthday.

"Happy birthday." Nicole glanced up at Alexander as he leaned against her desk.

"Thank you, but how did you find out?"

"Monique mentioned it when I told her to go home."

"Oh."

"Any special plans tonight?"

"No. Monique was talking about doing something, but then she became ill." She shrugged, hoping he would suggest taking her out, but he didn't.

"If I had known, I would have planned something for you here at work."

"It's no big deal." She hoped she sounded convincing. "Just another day."

Nicole seemed so sad. He wanted to pull her into his arms and comfort her. In fact, it took every ounce of self-restraint he possessed not to do just that in front of everyone.

Tonight would be the perfect time to give her the present he had been holding on to for weeks now. He'd go home after work, pick it up and bring it by her place at the surprise party Monique was now busy planning.

"Are you okay?" he asked.

"I'm just worried about Monique."

At her evident concern, he felt like a heel, but if he told her the truth, it would spoil her party, and he didn't want to do that.

"I'm sure she'll be okay." He covered her hand with his. "It's probably just a virus or something she ate."

"You're right." She smiled slightly. "I talked to her a little while ago, and she sounded much better."

"See." Alex squeezed her hand. "I'll bet by the time you get home, she'll be up and about."

"Knowing Monique, she will." Nicole smiled slightly.

"Sure she will. I'll let you get back to work." He stood and walked away before he was tempted to tell her what Monique had planned for her tonight—anything to wipe that sad look from her beautiful face.

She stared after him dejectedly, wondering why it didn't occur to him to ask her out tonight—not that she'd go with Monique not feeling well, but it would be nice to be asked. It would show that he cared.

She glanced at her sketch without seeing it. What could

be worse than being far away from home in a foreign country for her birthday, her roommate being sick and the man
she dreamed about nightly having no desire to spend this
special evening with her?

This was turning out to be the worst birthday ever.

"Monique, I'm home!" Nicole announced as she entered
their dark apartment around 7:30 that night.

"Surprise!" A multitude of voices yelled as a throng of
her coworkers jumped out to greet her and the lights were
switched on.

"What the…?" Nicole jumped and placed a hand to
her throat.

"Happy birthday!" Monique hugged her tightly, followed by Victor.

Nicole studied her roommate, who looked perfectly
healthy. She was smiling from ear to ear.

"Monique, you were faking," Nicole accused around
a laugh.

"For a good reason." Monique looked pleased with herself. "I had to arrange this impromptu party for you."

"I don't believe this." Nicole glanced around the gaily
decorated apartment. "You shouldn't have."

"Yes, I should have. Now go into your bedroom and
change into the festive duds I've laid out on your bed and
hurry back." Monique gave her a light shove, and Nicole
obeyed, laughing.

On her bed she found a lavender dress. After taking
a quick shower, she donned the light and airy creation,
which fit her feminine curves perfectly, from the long
sheer sleeves to the tight bodice and skirt that hit midthigh
and swayed when she moved. It was a sexy number that
Nicole wished Alexander could see her in. She wondered
if he knew about her party and if he'd be attending. She
hoped so.

Donning the matching strappy shoes, she then sprayed on some French perfume she had recently purchased. After finger combing her short hair into ordered disarray, she rejoined the party, which was in full swing.

"There's the birthday girl." Victor whistled and hugged her tight. "You look fabulous."

"Thanks." Nicole glanced down at her ensemble. "Monique, when did you buy this dress?"

"This afternoon after I left work. I've been so busy I'm ready to collapse!"

"The trouble you must have gone through." Nicole fought back happy tears.

"What trouble? This was pure fun. Besides, these guys love any excuse to party," Monique whispered, pulling Nicole into the center of the room.

When the doorbell rang, Monique asked her to get it, piquing Nicole's curiosity by predicting it was probably her other present. Nicole started to ask what she meant, but the bell rang again and she walked over and opened it with a smile.

"Alexander!" Her smile widened. "Hi."

"Happy birthday, Nicole," he responded, then handed her a red-and-white package with a frilly red bow.

"Thank you." She took the present and stood aside to allow him in. "Come on in and join the party."

"Thanks." He followed her inside.

Bless Monique—now her birthday was complete. No wonder he hadn't asked her out; he had known Monique was throwing this party. It all made perfect sense now, and the heaviness that had invaded her heart earlier completely vanished.

"Can I get you a drink?" Nicole asked.

"Sure, anything." He followed her to the set-up bar.

"Glad you could come, boss." Monique smiled as he

passed her and winked at Nicole, who shook her head tolerantly. Bless her matchmaking little heart!

"Thanks for inviting me," he answered Monique before continuing to the bar with Nicole.

"Aren't you going to open your present?" he asked when she handed him a drink.

"Would you like me to open it now?" She fingered the fluffy bow.

"Please." He watched her face as she carefully peeled back paper and ribbon, and her gasp of delight told him she was pleased.

She lifted the porcelain carousel music box she had admired weeks ago and raised teary eyes at him. "I don't believe you bought this for me," she whispered. "I went back to get it, and it was gone. I was crushed."

"I knew you liked it." He was pleased and unnerved by her reaction. "It's no big deal."

"It is a big deal." She kissed his cheek, holding him close for a few precious seconds. "Thank you."

"You're welcome." He coughed somewhat nervously, and to change the subject asked, "Would you like to dance?"

"I don't know."

He frowned. "What don't you know?"

"How's your back?"

"About ninety-five percent."

"Still trying for one hundred percent?"

"Yep, and I'm almost there," he promised. "So how about it?"

"Well…" She hesitated. "This music is so fast. Are you sure dancing won't hurt your back?" Midsong, the music suddenly turned nice and slow. She glanced across at Monique, who waved the remote in her hands. Nicole shook her head in exasperation and returned her focus to Alexander.

"Perfect timing." Alex held out his hand to her. He knew he shouldn't dance with her, but God, he needed to hold her in his arms, and dancing gave him the perfect excuse to do just that without being too obvious.

"That's my roomie." Nicole chuckled, allowing him to lead her onto the dance floor in the center of the room.

"I'm glad you're happier than you were earlier."

"I'll admit I was pretty sad."

"I wanted to tell you about the party, but Monique would have had my head."

"I'm glad you didn't. It was a wonderful surprise." She paused before adding, "I love my present. You must have gone back immediately and bought it."

"A couple of days after we saw it," he admitted.

"And you've had it all this time." She eyed him curiously. "Just waiting for the perfect time to give it to me?"

"Nicole, don't make more of it than it is."

She studied him closely. "What exactly is it?"

"A gift for an employee." That was a lame excuse and he knew it, but it was the only one he had to offer.

"An employee?" A perfectly arched eyebrow rose doubtfully. "Do you give all your employees expensive handmade music boxes?"

"Okay, point taken," he agreed. "Let's just say I wanted you to have it and leave it at that, okay?"

"All right, but I won't stop thinking about it," she promised and laughed when he sighed. "Being here in Paris with you has been the best time of my life."

"You mean working at Alexander's," he clarified.

"No, I said what I meant—being with *you*," she softly reiterated.

"Nicole…" His heart somersaulted at her easy, honest admission.

"Yes, Alexander?"

Oh, God, the sexy way she said his name stroked him in all the right places. He stared at her silently, fighting the need to fuse his lips to hers. Instead he pulled her a little closer, suddenly wishing the dance would never end, but it did, much too soon.

"Time for presents," someone proclaimed.

Nicole was reluctantly pulled out of his arms and steered onto the sofa, and presents were presented to her, which she dutifully opened. They were all lovely, yet none touched her as much as Alexander's. She glanced at her watch, saw it was a minute before 8:30 p.m. and hastily stood.

"Where are you going?" Monique asked.

"I have a video call scheduled with my family," Nicole said. "They'll skin me alive if I miss it."

"Okay." Monique nodded. "Hurry back."

"I will." She went to her bedroom to set up her PC.

Fifteen minutes later, she returned, wiping away a happy tear from her eye. She felt someone touch her arm and knew instinctively it was Alexander.

"Are you okay?" Alex asked.

"I'm fine. Just happy tears."

"Those are okay then," he said. "How about some cake?"

"I'd love some." She almost melted when his fingers naturally twined with hers as they walked over to the food tables.

"How's your family?"

"Wonderful." She smiled fondly. "I miss them."

"I'm sorry." He squeezed her hand comfortingly. "August will be here before you know it, and then you'll be reunited with them."

Instead of making her feel better, his words had the opposite effect. Yes, if all went well, she was scheduled to transfer to the New York office in August, which meant she would be going home, but it also meant she would be leaving Paris—and more importantly, him. She wasn't anywhere near ready to think of not having him in her life yet; she doubted she ever would be.

"That's true, but when I return to New York, I'll be leaving the people I care about here behind."

"You mean Monique?"

"And Victor." She paused and purposefully added, "And you especially."

"Nicole." He fidgeted uneasily. "I'm not someone you want to get involved with."

"Yes, you are," she softly countered, moving closer to him. "You really are."

"Hey, birthday girl," Victor interrupted them. "How about a dance?"

She glanced at Alexander, who seemed relieved and annoyed by the intrusion. She was torn between staying and continuing their serious conversation or going with Victor and enjoying her party. She decided to let Alexander think about her last statement.

"I thought you'd never ask." Nicole took Victor's outstretched hand and followed him onto the dance floor, leaving Alexander alone staring after them broodingly.

It was hours before guests began to reluctantly file out. Monique certainly knew how to throw a party. Alexander and Nicole found themselves alone in the apartment after Monique and Victor decided to go out for coffee.

"Well, those two were completely obvious," Alex said, smirking.

"Very," Nicole agreed, fingering her music box.

Alex sat down beside her on the sofa. "Was it a happy birthday?"

"One of the best. I thought it would be horrible because

I am so far away from my family, but all of you made it wonderful."

"I'm glad."

"I can't believe Monique organized this party in a few hours, or that she went through all this trouble for me."

"She loved every second of it," Alex promised. "She was hilarious making phone calls while feigning illness so you wouldn't be on to her."

"She completely fooled me."

"That means she did her job very well."

"She really did." Nicole placed a hand on his arm and slid closer to him.

"Nicole…"

"Shut up and kiss me, Alexander," she softly ordered. "That will make my birthday complete."

He smiled at her and lowered his head to comply. Their lips came together as if they had been made for that express purpose. He kissed her deeply, lingeringly, as he had wanted to do all night long. She melted against him, her soft curves effortlessly conforming to his hard muscles. One kiss led to another and another, until he wanted to rip the dress from her and bury himself in her soft fragrant skin.

They were on fire—both wanting nothing less than complete consummation of this devastating desire they shared. After endless minutes, Alex pulled back with difficulty, though his mouth still engaged in butterfly kisses with hers.

"She was a fool," Nicole whispered against his mouth.

"Who?" He forced his mouth from hers and stared into her warm eyes.

"The woman who hurt you."

"Who says I was hurt?"

"Your eyes do." She touched his cheek with her palm. "I'll never hurt you, Alexander."

It was scary how badly he wanted to believe her, and more frightening was the fact that a big part of him did believe her. He hadn't even known her for two months yet, so how she had successfully burrowed so far underneath his carefully crafted defenses he couldn't begin to understand.

"Do you believe me?"

"I believe it's time to go." He stood and walked to the door; she slowly followed. He stood with his back toward her for several long seconds before confessing, "There was this woman five years ago. Her name was Nina Laurent."

Nicole's heart thudded against her chest. He was going to confide in her about Nina. This was important and would mark a turning point in their relationship.

"Go on." At her soft invitation, he turned to face her.

"It was right after my parents died, and I was fighting with the board to be named CEO of Alexander's." He paused to gather his thoughts before continuing. "I was searching for allies at work and thought Nina was someone who believed in me and my ability to run the company."

"She didn't?"

"No. She was the worst mistake I've ever made." His eyes hardened. "She portrayed herself as someone I could trust, and long story short, she stole designs and sold them to my biggest competitor, and I almost lost the CEO appointment as a result."

"I'm so sorry." Nicole touched his arm to comfort him. "How could she betray you like that?"

"I was a fool for trusting her. It was my fault. I had too much going on and wasn't paying attention the way I should have been."

"You trusted the wrong person. We've all done that at one time or another."

"It's a mistake I don't plan to make again." *If* he allowed himself to trust anyone other than Victor, it would be Nicole, though.

"I understand why you're overly cautious with your heart, Alexander, but you *can* trust me. I hope you realize that one day."

He stared at her long and hard, trying to discern the truth of her statement. She had never given him any reason to mistrust her, but was he capable of trusting anyone completely again? He honestly didn't know.

"I should go."

"Thank you for telling me about Nina." She moved closer to him. "I know why you find it so hard to let anyone in, but this between us is not going to go away," she promised. "Believe me, I know. I've tried to make it, but it won't go away." At his telling silence she continued, "We're going to have to deal with the desire we feel—soon—or it's going to drive us crazy."

"Good night, Nicole." He opened the door without acknowledging the truth of her statement.

"Good night. Thank you again for my present."

"You're welcome." Before he could leave, she reached up and pressed her lips to his. He kissed her back ardently, crushing her body against his while his mouth pillaged for long satisfying seconds before finally pulling away with difficulty.

"See, it's not going away," she reiterated. He stared at her hungrily and seemed to be waging a silent war with himself before finally leaving without uttering another word.

Nicole sighed and closed the door. She finally knew what Nina Laurent had done to poison Alexander on relationships; she had betrayed him in the worst ways, personally and professionally. Nicole vowed to show him she was nothing like Nina and that he could believe in her and in them. She would do it no matter how long it took because anything less wasn't an option.

Chapter 13

It was the night of their in-house fashion show. A few very prominent names in fashion had been invited, but no press because this show was a precursor to their big event in August, and they didn't want any of the designs being leaked. The affair was top secret.

The fashion show and dinner were being held at the luxurious Le Meurice Hotel. Nicole had never seen anything so beautifully ornate in her life, and she had been to some high-end parties in the United States. She fought to keep her mouth from gaping open as she entered the room on Alexander's arm.

One of the hotel's large banquet rooms had been transformed into a runway at one end, while numerous dinner tables covered in white linen took up the other end. The tables were set with the finest crystal and china, with pale pink and white roses as the centerpieces. Gold-and-white tapestry chairs rounded each table.

Sparkling crystal chandeliers with gold accents hung

from the high ceilings, and strategically placed stone columns elegantly partitioned the room. The crowning glory was the crystal clear ceiling-to-floor windows, allowing for a breathtaking view of the twinkling lights of the city.

Nicole clung to Alexander's arm as they passed by representatives from two of Paris's most famous fashion houses. He squeezed her hand and gave her a comforting smile, which allayed some, but not all, of her apprehension.

Alexander looked handsome as ever, dressed in a black tux, crisp white shirt and black bow tie. She had not seen him formally dressed, and the sight of him when he had picked her up had almost rendered her speechless. The way his eyes dilated when he saw her had informed her he approved of her appearance, as well.

"Don't be nervous," he ordered.

"How can I not be?" she whispered back. "This is a fashion lover's dream. My God, some of the top names in fashion are here!" He laughed at her obvious exuberance, and she felt like poking him in the side.

"They're just people, Nicole," he promised. "They put their pants on one leg at a time."

"That's easy for you to say. You're one of them," she softly accused, and he smiled.

"I guess I am, but that just proves my point. I'm not scary, am I?"

"No, not now that I know you, but when we first met…" she trailed off.

"Come on, I wasn't that bad, was I?" He smiled down at her.

"No comment."

"Ouch!" He treated her to an exaggerated wounded expression, which made her laugh.

"Sorry," she apologized. Her feet faltered as she realized where he was leading her. "Oh, my God, we're not going to talk to the Prada team, are we?"

"Yes, we are." He pulled her along. "Just flash that gorgeous smile of yours, and they'll be the ones who are awestruck."

"But Alexander…"

"No buts. It's showtime!" He brightly announced. "I promise I'll stay right by your side."

"Promise?"

"Cross my heart." He made an *X* over his heart with his forefinger.

"Okay, but if you leave me alone with them, I promise you I'm going to faint and embarrass you terribly."

"No chance of that. I'm not going anywhere." His easy promise reassured and thrilled her, and she relaxed a little as they approached the haute couture designer's table.

He stayed by her side as they worked the room—not because he had promised her, but because there was nowhere else he would rather be. Besides, he had no intention of giving another man the privilege of her company tonight; he selfishly wanted her all to himself.

They shared a table with Monique, Victor, several other designers from Alexander's and two members of the board. Once seated among friends, Nicole relaxed perceptibly. As Alex had predicted, she charmed everyone who came in contact with her, and he watched with admiration as she spoke knowledgeably about Alexander's proposed fashion lines with the members of the board, one of whom just happened to be the man who had given him a terrible time in his bid to become acting CEO of Alexander's. Nicole effortlessly had him eating out of her hands within minutes. She was spectacular.

When he had picked Nicole up tonight, he had been floored by how gorgeous she looked dressed in a knockout black full-length lace sheath, a figure-hugging gown from Alexander's timeless classics line. The gown left her arms and a huge swath of her back bare. It was cut in a modest V-neck in the front and plunging V in the back.

She wore opera-length black gloves, a matching triple-row pearl-and-diamond bracelet and choker and drop earrings. Her hair was parted on one side and slicked down, showing her precision cut to perfection in neat line and framing her gorgeous face. To say she looked stunning was an understatement, and from the masculine eyes that had followed her earlier when they worked the room, he wasn't the only one who thought so.

After dinner, his knuckleheaded brother whisked her away to the dance floor before he could object. Now Alexander stood across the room, leaning against a column, broodingly watching the two of them. Victor effortlessly twirled *his* Nicole around the floor before pulling her close again. She smiled and then laughed at something he said, and her fabulous smile resided on her lips for the entirety of their dance.

They appeared to be having a blast—a fact that irked him to no end. Logically, Alex knew he was being stupid, but logic had nothing to do with the insane streak of jealousy that rushed through him as he watched Nicole in another man's arms—even though that man was his baby brother.

He was more than ready to burst from the frustration of trying to keep a lid on his explosive desire for her. With each day, he wanted her more. He knew all the reasons for not getting romantically involved with her, but frankly they seemed inconsequential and silly when compared to the simple pleasure of being in her presence.

As he continued to watch, someone cut in on Victor, who relinquished his hold on Nicole. She accepted the other man's offer to dance with a smile. Alexander's blood boiled when she went into his arms. Dammit, seeing her with Victor was one thing, but having yet another man touching her was intolerable.

"Bro, who are you plotting to murder?" Victor chuckled as he walked over to stand beside him

"No one." Alex snatched a glass of champagne from a passing waiter and downed it in one gulp.

"Alex, they're just dancing."

"I don't know what you mean." Alex returned his empty glass and took another full one.

"Sure you don't." Victor also picked up a glass of champagne. "She's a great dancer."

"Yes, I know she is."

"I could dance with her all night," Victor continued. "It looks like her current dance partner feels the same way, and I know for a fact there are a number of other guys waiting their turn to find out."

"Excuse me." Having had enough, Alex moved into action.

"That's right, bro. Go get your woman," Victor approved, prompting his brother to stop long enough to smirk at him before continuing on to do as he suggested. "Bravo, big brother. Bravo." Victor grinned as Alex set off.

Alex pointedly tapped the man dancing with Nicole on the shoulder, who reluctantly released her but not before kissing her hand and thanking her for the dance. Alex's mouth thinned, and he waited impatiently for the man to get lost.

"I see you're enjoying yourself." His sarcastic tone seemed lost on Nicole, who smiled at him dazzlingly.

"I feel like Cinderella." She laughed. "I'm having a marvelous time."

"You look like a princess," he said. "You're very beautiful tonight."

"Thank you." Her hand moved higher on his shoulder, toward his neck. "I could dance all night long."

"So I've noticed."

She seemed to notice how tense he was. "What's wrong, Alexander?"

"Nothing."

"It's not nothing." She frowned and then smiled. "You're not jealous because I've been dancing with other men, are you?"

"Of course not."

She chuckled and Alexander frowned at her, which increased her laughter.

"What's so funny?"

"Nothing." At his intense stare, she relented and elaborated, "I was just thinking about something Victor said when we danced. He's so funny."

"Yeah, he's a riot." He glanced away from her.

"Alexander." At her chiding voice, he returned his disturbed eyes to her amused ones.

"What?"

"I've told you before, Victor and I are just friends," she softly reminded him. "More important, you know your brother wouldn't do anything to hurt you—and neither would I."

He stared into her sincere eyes and had the grace to feel ashamed. *Why am I acting like such an idiot?* After silently berating himself for his behavior, he sighed. "I know."

"Do you?" She grinned as a faint smile spread across his handsome face and he visibly relaxed. "Good."

"I don't have any right to be jealous where you're concerned anyway."

"Yes, you do," she quickly contradicted. "As far as I'm concerned, you alone have *every* right."

"Nicole…"

The announcement that the fashion show was about to begin halted his words. He was relieved because he didn't know what he had been about to confess, but whatever it was, he felt it was best left unsaid.

They stopped dancing, and he escorted her back to their table. The lights dimmed and the show started. She and Alexander smiled at each other when the gown they had designed together received thunderous applause. It was the best night of his life because Nicole was by his side. In a few short months, she had filled a void in his lonely life, and he honestly didn't know how to stop her from becoming even more embedded in his heart—honestly, he didn't know if he had the strength to try.

Hours later, after a highly successful show, Alex and Nicole were in his Ferrari speeding away from the hotel, having declined numerous invitations to go out and continue the night's celebration. She was disappointed that he was taking her home because she didn't want the evening to end, but his next words delighted her.

"Would you like to go back to my place for a nightcap?" He glanced at her briefly but intensely.

"Yes," she accepted without hesitation and ran her hand lightly up and down his arm. "Did I tell you how good you look in this tuxedo?"

He smiled but kept his attention on the road. "No, you didn't."

"My bad." She trailed a gloved nail down his clean-shaven cheek. "You look amazing in this tux."

"Nicole." He groaned her name as her fingers caressed his chin.

"Hmm?"

"I'm trying to concentrate on driving."

"And?" She gasped when his teeth nipped her finger as it outlined his lower lip.

"I can't with you touching me."

"Okay." She slid her fingers away from his flesh and

sat back in her seat. "I'll try to keep my hands to myself, but Alexander?"

"Yes."

"It's going to be very, very hard," she whispered.

"Did you enjoy the show?"

"Yes." She sighed happily. "I still can't believe I was in the same room with some of the biggest names in fashion."

"One day they'll be saying the same thing about you."

"Thank you." His words meant the world to her.

"Just speaking the truth." He returned her smile.

For the remainder of the ride, they purposefully kept the conversation light and inconsequential. They arrived at his house a little after midnight. Alexander unlocked the door and followed her inside.

The hallway was immediately illuminated, and at her curious look he explained, "The entire house is wired with smart lights. They come on when they detect movement in a room."

She looked thoroughly impressed. "That's so high tech."

"It's useful." He chuckled.

Taking her lace wrap, he placed it over a nearby chair. Then he kissed her neck lingeringly. She moved a gloved hand behind her to cup his cheek as she tilted her head to the side, giving his welcome mouth greater access. He made a symphony of kissing her neck until she turned in his arm, and their mouths gravitated together. They kissed long and deep before he broke contact.

"Why don't you wait in the living room while I get the wine?" he suggested.

She was on the verge of telling him she didn't want any wine but nodded in agreement and walked into the living room, smiling when the lights switched on automatically. She had just sat down on the leather sofa when he returned carrying a bottle of champagne and two flutes.

He popped the cork and poured the bubbly liquid, handing a full glass to her.

"Thank you." She held her glass up in a toast. "To new beginnings." He hesitated before lifting his glass and clinking it with hers.

"To new beginnings." They drank and stared deeply into each other's eyes. He sighed heavily and was compelled to confess, "Nicole, I'm no good at relationships."

"I don't believe that," she softly replied.

"Trust me—it's true." He took another swig of his champagne.

"Then why did you bring me here?"

"Because…because I…" He raked his fingers through his hair in frustration. He had brought her here because he wanted and needed her, but did he have a right to take her when he knew he wasn't a man who could offer her the kind of relationship she expected or deserved?

"You know what I think?" Without waiting for his reply she continued, "I think you've been dating the wrong women."

"Maybe there is no right woman for me," he responded.

"Now you've done it." She smiled sexily.

"What?"

"I can't stand negativism, so I have to prove how wrong you are."

"You *have* to?" he asked, amusement dancing in his eyes.

"Mmm-hmm."

She set down her glass, moved closer and placed a hand on his hard thigh; he jumped as a jolt of electricity shot through him, eyes locking on hers. She shivered as she looked into the depths of his eyes, leaning fully against him, a gloved hand caressing his cheek.

He touched her face and before he knew it, they were

kissing ravenously, as if their very lives depended on never breaking physical contact. He pulled her closer and reclined onto the sofa with her lying on top of him. Hands caressed the bare skin of her back fervently, relishing in the soft, warm feel of her before moving up her sides to her front, teasing her nipples through the thin lace of her dress. His fingers itched to peel her out of the figure-hugging gown and rain kisses down the length of her delectable body.

They engaged in another heated series of kisses. His hardness pressed against her lower stomach, and she groaned in anticipation. Her fingers fisted in his hair, her eyes tightly closed.

When he pulled away and sat up, she ended up on his lap, in perfect position to rain kisses along his rugged jaw before nibbling at his ear.

"Nicole, stop."

"No," she refused, settling her mouth at the base of his throat. "Alexander, why don't you stop fighting the inevitable?"

His hands forced her mouth away from his flesh as he simultaneously slid her from his lap. They stared at each other for long seconds. She framed his face with her hands and met him in a searing kiss until he pried his mouth away from hers.

"We shouldn't be doing this." He valiantly tried to infuse some measure of sanity into this maddening situation.

"This is long overdue," she whispered. "The way we feel about each other gets stronger every day, and we're going to explode if we keep fighting it."

He considered her words, which were one hundred percent true. Coming to a long-overdue conclusion, he stood and pulled her upright until she stood beside him.

"I know it isn't going away," he finally agreed.

"So what are you going to do about it?" she challenged.

His answer was to scoop her up into his arms and carry her into his bedroom. The room was dark until one overhead lamp switched on, softly illuminating the room. He sat her down beside the bed, hands traveling over her arms and shoulders. Staring into her alluring eyes the entire time, he slowly removed one glove then the other before divesting her of her jewelry and finally unzipping her dress.

"Nicole, are you sure?" His fingers danced up and down her bare spine.

"I've never been more certain about anything." Honest eyes bore into his burning ones. "I want you, Alexander."

He paused for an eternity before admitting, "I want you, too."

"Then take me," she invited.

Slowly, savoring every second, he peeled her dress off, allowing it to pool at her feet. Ravenous eyes feasted on every centimeter of exposed brown skin. She was a work of art, but better because she was flesh and blood and all his.

"You're so beautiful," he marveled.

"I feel beautiful when you look at me."

"You are, inside and out," he said, pulling her into arms that ached to hold her.

She wrapped her arms around his neck, pressed closer still and pulled his mouth down to hers. She rubbed against him until his arms tightened around her, stilling her. His mouth grew harder, more insistent, and hers was just as forceful as they familiarized themselves again with every secret treasure their lips and tongues uncovered.

"You have on too many clothes," she complained against his mouth.

"Why don't you help me out with that?" he suggested around a smile, and she gladly complied, unbuttoning his shirt, which he shrugged out of, along with his jacket, tie and finally his pants.

Then they were on the bed, naked bodies pressed close.

The marvelous differences between the textures of their skin and the composition of their bodies felt wonderful—where he was solid, she was soft and yielding, and where he bulged and protruded, she dipped and curved, and she cushioned him perfectly in all the right places.

Before he completely lost his mind, he rolled away from her, opened a bedside drawer and pulled out a foil package. She kissed his shoulders and broad back while her fingers spread across his chest and abdomen. He donned the condom in record time and then faced her again to feast on her fragrant skin while her hands touched him all over. He was dying from her feverish touch and from his monumental need.

"God, Nicole." He nipped at her lips. "I have to have you now."

"Yes," she groaned, arching against him.

"I can't be gentle," he thickly warned.

"Who asked for gentle? Just take me," she ordered.

Her soft body wrapped around his, and he knew heaven was almost within his grasp. He couldn't stop even if he wanted to, and Lord knew he didn't want to. He pushed into her. She welcomed him without hesitation. He wanted this to last forever, but he knew it wouldn't—it had been too long since he had been with a woman, and he had spent too many long, lonely nights dreaming of being with this one.

Her eyes glazed with passion, matching his. As they moved together effortlessly in perfect sync, she took him higher than he had ever been taken before. Every inch of her melted against him as if that was what she had been made for. Oh, God, it was so good; nothing had ever felt so right.

"Nicole," he groaned against her mouth.

"Alexander." She sighed his name before he took her mouth in a searing kiss—and much too soon, but just in time, the dam burst, flooding them both with wave after wave of blissful release.

Alex strummed his fingers lightly up and down Nicole's shoulder and arm as they lay together trying to regain their breath and bearings. She felt so good against him. Incredible. He wanted to absorb her into his body. She made him feel special—needed, wanted and alive. With her he was vulnerable—something he hadn't allowed himself to be for a long, long time, but at this moment, it didn't seem to matter.

He didn't want to want her, but want her he did; more than that, he craved her, and now that he had made her his, he doubted that feeling would lessen. And that saddened him because he knew what they had, no matter how good at this moment, wouldn't last; relationships never did.

Nicole's satiated body lay half-across Alexander's, her head resting on his chest, eyes closed with a blissful smile on her face.

"How do you feel?" Alexander asked her.

"Perfect." Curious fingers traced lazy patterns in the light hair covering his chest. "How do you feel?"

"Perfect." He echoed her sentiments, and she smiled.

"Alexander, has it ever felt like this for you before?"

"Like what?" He pulled her closer.

"Like you're dying and being born at the same time?" He was quiet as he digested her words that completely summed up his feelings.

"No, it never has," he slowly confessed.

"Not for me either." Lifting her head, she stared at him with an emotion he didn't dare name. "I guess that should tell us something."

"It tells me that I want you in a way I've never wanted anyone else." He outlined her face with his fingers.

"That's enough for now." She kissed his lips lightly before returning her head to his chest.

* * *

What they had just shared was what lovemaking was all about. Alexander had just done things to her, elicited responses and feelings from her that she hadn't thought herself capable of. Nothing had ever felt so right. Now residing in her lover's arms with her body and soul purring happily in the warm afterglow of their intimate union, she allowed herself to admit what she had known for weeks— she had finally found that special someone to share her life with in Alexander James.

Chapter 14

"Alexander, where are we going?"

Wearing one of his T-shirts, she walked slowly in front of him, his hand covering her eyes. She'd rather still be in bed with him. It was 5:00 a.m. and they hadn't slept all night, which was fine with her; she wasn't the least bit tired.

"You'll see," he whispered in her ear.

"I can't see anything," she joked.

"That's because I want to surprise you." He kissed her neck. "We're almost there."

"Where?" He didn't answer her, just continued guiding her.

"Okay, now you can look." He removed his hand.

"Oh, Alexander!" She glanced at the free-standing sunken tub filled with bubbles, innumerable candles of all shapes and sizes placed strategically around the room illuminating it.

"So." He turned her into his arms and bobbed his eyebrows. "Wanna try out the tub with me?"

"Oh, yes." She ran her palms up his bare chest, arms encircling his neck. "You know I do."

She raised her arms, and he obligingly pulled the T-shirt over her head. She faced him, unabashed, as his appreciative eyes, followed by his reverent hands, roamed over her nude body.

"You're so gorgeous."

"I'm yours," she promised.

"All mine." He smiled happily, picking her up and setting her in the tub. He quickly discarded his pajama bottoms and joined her, pulling her into his arms, her back reclining against his chest.

"This is heaven."

"It is," he agreed, soapy hands roaming slowly over her. "Your skin is so soft."

"I love the way you touch me."

"I love touching you," he growled in her ear.

"Then don't stop." She covered his hands as they caressed her breasts. "Mmm, that feels so good."

"Yes, you do." He lightly bit into her neck.

"This is the only way to bathe." She closed her eyes with a satisfied sigh.

"I completely agree."

"Any regrets?"

"No," he quickly assured her. "What about you?"

"Absolutely none." She raised her hand behind her to caress his cheek as he nibbled on her earlobe. "Well, maybe one," she corrected on a sigh.

"What's that?"

"That we didn't do this sooner."

He chuckled against her ear, sending delicious shivers down her spine.

"We were fighting a losing battle, weren't we?"

"I told you so."

"You were right."

* * *

Alex was absolutely content at this moment, but he couldn't help wondering how long that would last, and more important, how long *they* would last.

"I wish we could stay like this forever."

"The water would get cold," he joked, forcing negative thoughts from his mind.

"I mean just the two of us in our own little world," she said.

"So do I," he agreed.

She turned sideways and laid her cheek on his shoulder. Their lips gravitated together, and as usual, fire combusted. Her hands explored his chest and abs, running up and down his muscles, enjoying the feel of him. When her hand slipped beneath the water, he groaned against her mouth before breaking off their kiss. She moaned in protest, seeking his mouth again, which he evaded, along with her stroking hands.

Pushing her slightly away he stood, forced her to do the same, led her out of the tub and sat her on the sparkling white counter across the room. He grabbed a condom out of the cabinet, hurriedly rolled it on and was back standing in front of her before she could blink.

She gave a sultry smile, leaned forward and feasted on his chest and neck until his hands cradled her face and pulled her mouth to his. He couldn't get enough of her addictive mouth; he doubted he ever would. He could get off just by kissing her.

Her arms encircled his neck, and his hands stroked her calves before hooking her legs around his hips as he sank into her. She gasped against his mouth and pressed closer; their wet, slick bodies felt incredible against each other's.

Alexander's pace was slow, and he refused to be rushed even when her soft, warm body, urged him to move faster.

He wanted to savor every second of loving the incredible woman in his arms, and he was going to do just that. Nicole seemed to sense his resolve and gave in to his unhurried pace.

"No, look at me, Nicole," he ordered against her mouth when her eyes slid closed in response to his body's intimate stroking of hers. With difficulty, she obeyed his hoarse command, lids half opening again. "That's it. Keep looking at me, baby."

They maintained eye contact, stayed completely focused, staring deeply, kissing softly, breath intermingling as one.

Nicole felt stripped raw emotionally as she beheld the naked passion that burned in Alexander's eyes. Her nails dug into his solid shoulders before moving to his flexing back. His hands journeyed down her back, resting on her hips, holding her exactly where he wanted her as their bodies continued their passionate yet unhurried dance.

She never thought anything could feel more perfect or more wonderful than when they had made love earlier, but he proved her wrong. Time stood still, and the pleasure built to unbearable heights until she was whimpering against Alex's caressing mouth. Unable to keep her eyes open another second, she closed them tightly and started to shake—softly at first, and then with increasing urgency as the flames of their desire ignited, blazed and destroyed.

Alexander groaned against her mouth, and his body tensed as taut as a stringed bow. He crushed her to him as he too reached that special place with her that only lovers can share—a world without reason, giving way to blissful madness before finally arriving at their destination of utter fulfillment.

* * *

Nicole awoke to the wonderful feeling of kisses being rained down her shoulders and back. Reverent hands massaged her breasts, fingers tweaking her nipples.

"Mmm, Alexander." She sighed, opening her eyes to sunlight streaming through the bedroom windows.

"Morning." His voice was muffled by her skin.

"Good morning." She turned to face him and snuggled against his chest. "What a wonderful way to wake up."

"I'm not letting you out of this bed all day."

"Thank God it's Saturday." She smiled. "I'm all yours."

"It's after ten," he murmured against her mouth. "Are you hungry?"

"Starved," she said.

"Okay." He kissed her soundly and then threw back the covers and got up.

"Where are you going?" She enjoyed the view as she reclined in bed.

"To get you some food." He bent down and kissed her again. "You're going to need your strength."

"Have mercy." She fanned herself with her hand and plopped back against the pillows.

"No mercy for you, my love," he wickedly promised, bending down to retrieve his pajama bottoms and donning them before sauntering out of the room.

When he returned about twenty minutes later, she was replacing the phone on the nightstand.

"Who were you talking to?" He sat beside her and placed the tray on his lap.

"Monique. I was letting her know not to expect me today."

"Or tonight either, I hope." He kissed her bare shoulder.

"I didn't want to presume." She smiled.

"The hell you say!" She giggled at his fake outrage before he kissed her soundly, breaking the kiss before they got carried away. "First, food."

She eyed the food-laden tray. "It looks wonderful. You're a good cook."

"I had to be. Victor can't boil water, but he loves to eat."

"You're such a good brother." Her fingers caressed his cheek.

"It's a thankless job, but someone's gotta do it."

"You do it well."

"Thanks." He plopped a strawberry into her mouth.

"Mmm, that's delicious." She rolled her eyes heavenward and picked up another berry.

"Let me taste." He bypassed the berry in her hands, tasting the one in her mouth instead. "You're right, so sweet."

"Have some more," Nicole offered. He placed a berry between her lips and covered the other half with his mouth. When their lips met, they kissed ravenously, and when they pulled apart, they were breathless.

"Try the mango." He offered her a slice, and she happily accepted it. They spent the next half hour feeding each other—between kisses and caresses.

"What?" she asked when she noticed he was grinning at her.

"I love watching you eat." His smile widened as she plopped the last forkful of eggs into her mouth, chewed and swallowed before sighing contentedly.

"I told you I enjoy food, and that—" she glanced at the now empty tray "—was delicious."

"Thank you. Have you had enough, or do you want seconds?"

She patted her stomach. "I'm stuffed."

"Well." He removed the tray and placed it on the floor. "How about we work some of those calories off?"

"I believe in exercise." She took his hand and pulled him down beside her.

"Me, too." He pulled the sheet away from her. "Especially the kind that requires a partner."

"Oh, yes." Nicole pushed him onto his back and straddled his hips. "I'm a team player."

Her mouth made a beeline for his neck. Her teeth nibbled at his flesh while her fingers massaged his chest and shoulders.

"Oh, God, that's good," he moaned, hand behind her head holding her close.

"I'm just getting started," she promised, tongue trailing down his jaw.

"Oh, damn!" He groaned as she took love bites out of his chest.

The phone began ringing, which Alex intended to ignore until he realized by the ringtone it was his brother calling. If he didn't answer, Victor would come over, and he didn't want his time with Nicole to be interrupted.

"Babe, can you hand me my cell?"

"I'm busy." Her voice was muffled against his flesh.

"Okay." He laughed, rolling her onto her side so that he could reach the phone. She pushed him onto his back as her mouth continued feasting on his flesh.

"Hey, Vic." He half listened as Nicole's sweet mouth treated him to pleasure. "No, I'm busy today. Hmm? No, not tonight either." His hand on the back of her head urged her on, and he felt her smile against his stomach. "Busy Sunday, too." He closed his eyes as her lips and tongue traced light patterns across his sculpted abs.

"You're not alone, are you?" Victor accused, laughing.

"Not that it's any of your business, but no I'm not."

"Are you with Nicole?" Alex laughed at the hopeful voice and then groaned as Nicole's hands caressed his sex.

"Victor, I've gotta go," he snapped.

"Answer my question, or I might just show up unannounced," Victor threatened.

"Yes," Alex quickly admitted. "Satisfied?"

"Not as much as you obviously are." Victor laughed.

"You don't know the half of it." Alex chuckled, which turned to a groan as Nicole's tongue delved into his belly button.

"Enjoy yourself, bro."

"I intend to." He tossed the phone to the floor and pulled Nicole back up to fuse his lips with hers.

"What did Victor want?" she asked around a kiss.

"Just checking up on me."

"That's sweet of him." She laughed as he rolled her onto her back.

"Mmm-hmm." He feathered light caresses across her collarbone. "But I know of something even sweeter."

"What?" Her hands fisted in his hair.

"This." His hot mouth engulfed a breast, and all talking was quickly forgotten.

"Remind me why I let you coax me out of bed?" Nicole asked as they entered her apartment early Saturday evening.

"Because you need some clothes other than an evening gown."

"Not if we stayed in bed."

"Don't worry, we'll get back there." He pulled her into his arms. "But first I have plans for you that require clothes."

"Okay." She kissed him before moving out of his arms. "Monique, are you here?" She walked to her room, which was empty. "I guess she's out, which means we have the place to ourselves." Nicole smiled seductively, walking back to Alexander and running her palms up, down and then under his black T-shirt before pressing her body against his.

"Behave." He removed her hands from underneath his shirt. "I have plans for us."

"What are they?" She lightly bit his chin. "Can I change your mind?"

"Oh, you could easily change my mind," he agreed, stepping away from her. "But I won't let you. Now go and change into something casual and comfortable."

"Okay." He chuckled at her disappointed sigh.

"I promise I'll make it up to you later, baby."

"Oh, yes, you will," she threatened over her shoulder before disappearing into her bedroom.

When she returned a little later, she was dressed in a flowing white, midthigh-length summery dress and matching white sandals. Alexander whistled his approval. She scribbled Monique a note to let her know she'd be back Sunday night, and they left.

When they reached his car, he steered her to the driver's side.

"What are you doing?"

"You're driving."

"Me?" Her eyes widened in shock. "Alexander, I can't."

"Yes, you can." He opened the door and helped her inside before walking around and getting into the passenger seat. "Just press the ignition button, and we're on our way."

"I've never driven a Ferrari before." Nicole nervously did as instructed.

"I told you I'd teach you," he reminded her, buckling his seat belt and motioning for her to do the same. "It's just like any other car."

"Yeah, right."

"Okay, it's more powerful and more expensive," he admitted. "Come on, babe. Where's your sense of adventure?"

Put like that, how could she refuse?

"Okay." She pulled out into traffic. "Here we go."

"That's my girl."

"Yes, I am," she said as they sped away.

"How do you like her?" he asked about thirty minutes later.

"She's something. I could definitely get used to her."

"I told you so." His hand covered her knee before sliding upward under the skirt of her dress to caress her inner thigh.

"Stop that," Nicole chided.

"Hmm?" His fingers rubbed her skin urgently.

"If you don't stop that, I'm going to wreck your car," she breathlessly warned.

"It's insured." His hand snaked higher up her inner thigh.

"Alexander James, stop it." She moaned the order.

"Okay." He slowly slid his hand from her soft skin.

"Oh, I miss your touch," she complained, and he laughed.

"You told me to stop."

"I know, but I still miss it."

"I'll touch you all you want once we get to our destination."

"Which is where?"

"It's a secret." At her pretty pout he relented. "We're going outside of the city into the country. We're about two hours away."

"Let's see how fast this baby can go, shall we?" Nicole flashed a challenging smile.

"Go for it," Alexander agreed and laughed when she depressed the accelerator and the car shot forward.

An hour and a half later, she screeched to a halt at Alexander's instructions. They were in a secluded meadow in the French countryside. They hadn't seen or passed a soul on the deserted roads. Lush green trees littered the side of the highway and the vast grassy fields beyond.

"How'd I do?" She turned in her seat after killing the engine.

"You handled her beautifully," he praised.

"She's a joy to drive. I see why Victor loves to borrow her."

"Because he's cheap. I'll probably have to break down and buy him one for his birthday."

"What a good brother."

"Come on." He kissed her quick and hard before exiting the car and walking around to open her door and helping her out.

"Where are we going?"

"You'll see."

She laughed at his mysterious smile. They walked hand in hand down a pebble path for a short while before disappearing into a grove of trees, where a picnic awaited them.

"How did you do this?"

"I have my ways," he mysteriously replied.

"You are too good to me."

"There's no such thing." He kissed her hand as they walked over and sat down on the red blanket.

"You know, it looks like rain," she said, glancing at the dark gray sky.

"It's not in the forecast today." Alex opened the wine, poured two glasses and offered one to her.

"Okay, if you say so." She tasted her wine and eyed the contents of the picnic basket before spreading them out on the blanket. She had no sooner set everything out than a drop of rain fell on the back of her hand. She glanced at Alexander and smiled.

"It's not going to rain," he predicted, feeding her a wedge of cheese.

Another drop of water splattered on his forearm, followed by another and another. Alex sighed, and Nicole giggled.

"I told you it was going to rain."

"You're not afraid of a little rain, are you?"

"Certainly not." She kissed him. The rain began to fall harder and harder, and they pulled apart, laughing. "We're going to get drenched if we stay out here, though."

"So?" He bobbed his eyebrows. "I love how you look wet."

"Oh, really?"

"Mmm-hmm." He pulled her to her feet. "But I don't want you to catch cold." His hands roamed over her. "I have plans for you, and being sick would put a serious damper on them."

"Well in that case, let's move this party to the car."

"I'm with you." They hurriedly gathered their things and made a mad dash for the Ferrari, getting inside just as a torrential downpour started.

"Come over here." Alexander beckoned her into the passenger seat with him.

"What do you have in mind?" She straddled his lap, resting her back against the dash.

"You'll see." He smiled wickedly, pulling down the back zip of her dress before peeling the damp garment down to her waist.

"Why, Mr. James, I'm not that kind of a girl." Her hands snaked under his T-shirt before pulling it over his head. "You think you can get me to make out with you on our first picnic?"

"I think I can." He confidently smiled.

"Nope." She shook her head and kissed him soundly. "It's not gonna be that easy."

"I think your resolve is weak," he murmured against her mouth. "Let's see what I can do to change your mind."

"I'm open to negotiation."

"Here's my opening salvo." Hands ran over her exposed skin, squeezing her lace-covered breasts. Then he kissed her collarbone and chest.

"Very good, but I'm still not budging."

"How about this?" He deftly removed her bra and took a round breast in his mouth before switching to the other.

"You're a very talented negotiator."

"Am I convincing you?"

"Mmm." She held his head closer to her humming skin. "Yes, but I still need more."

"Oh, I've got more," he promised, his teeth worrying her nipple. His seeking hands removed her panties, and then he pulled a condom out of his pocket and she took it from him.

"Good, because I need all that you've got."

She scooted back on his thighs as she unbuttoned his jeans, and together they sheathed him as they kissed ravenously. His hands on her hips lifted her and set her back down on his lap, effortlessly joining their bodies into one. They groaned in ecstasy.

The rain now pelted down on the car, echoing the frantic beating of their hearts as they scratched the ever-present itch of their combustible desire. His hands guided her hips as his mouth feasted on her breasts. Her fingers anchored in his hair, holding him close to her. Echoing sighs and groans filled the car as they gave everything they had and took all each had to give.

They held tight, waiting for the tremors to subside, which took some time. Their harsh breathing grew steadier, and the rain was now a soft purr, its fury having been spent like the two lovers who were still pressed close.

"Your persuasive skills are exceptional," Nicole breathlessly said against his neck.

"In that case, could I persuade you to…?" He whispered his demand in her ear and then pulled back to smile wickedly at her.

"Oh, God, yes," she groaned, meeting his hungry mouth halfway in a searing kiss.

Chapter 15

Sunday night came much too quickly to suit Nicole. It was the best weekend she had ever spent, and she was dreading having it end. He took her home late Sunday night, a little before midnight, as they had tried to prolong their time together as much as they could.

At her door, Alexander pulled Nicole into his arms. His hands caressed her back while hers rested on his sturdy shoulders.

"I don't want to let you go," he admitted around a kiss.

"I don't want to go either." Her arms tightened around his neck, and her mouth sought out his for longer contact.

"You'd better go in." His actions belied his words as his arms tightened around her waist, and his mouth engulfed hers once more. "I don't know how I'm going to keep my hands off you at work," Alex confessed a short while later.

"It's going to be hard for me, too." She ran her fingers through his hair as her lips played with his.

"We need to get in our fill while we can." His hands roamed over her familiarly.

"I don't think that's going to be possible." She pressed closer, thrilling at the feel of his hard body against hers.

"Let's give it a shot."

"Let's," she agreed, pressing her mouth to his.

He kissed her silly, but pulled back before they lost control and gave the other tenants quite a show. His lips still played with hers, though.

"We'd better stop."

"Yes, I know." She pushed slightly out of his arms. "I miss you already."

"Miss you, too," he echoed. But he pulled her back against him and kissed her, long, hot and thoroughly. "Good night." He caressed her cheek before turning and leaving while he could.

Nicole fought the urge to run after Alexander. Instead she sighed and then went into her apartment. She was surprised to see Monique curled up on the sofa with a throw over her lap.

"Hey, roomie."

"Hey." Nicole managed a small smile. "What are you doing up so late?"

"I was watching a movie." Monique switched off the television. "Why so sad? I expected you to be floating on cloud nine."

"I am." Nicole flopped down on the sofa beside her. "I just miss Alexander."

"Oh, boy, you've got it bad."

"I do," she agreed. "Monique…"

"What?"

"You'll think I'm crazy."

"No, I won't." She squeezed Nicole's hand and urged her on. "Tell me."

Taking a deep breath, she admitted, "I think I'm falling in love with Alexander."

"I think you have been for a while now."

"You're right," Nicole softly acknowledged. "How did this happen when I wasn't even remotely looking for it?"

"That's when Cupid strikes," Monique teased. "Didn't you know that?"

Nicole smiled but remained silent. She hoped and prayed that Cupid had struck Alexander, too.

Nicole had never been happier for a Monday morning to arrive because Sunday night was absolutely miserable. She'd tossed and turned, unable to sleep without Alexander. When she arrived at work Monday morning, he was walking around the designer area, inspecting sketches. She secretly suspected he was waiting for her to arrive, which pleased her very much.

Her heart flipped in her chest when their eyes met as she made her way to her desk. He gazed at her longingly before his eyes became hooded and professional. She understood, but how she wanted to run into his arms, longing to feel his strong, warm embrace.

"Good morning, Nicole." To keep from touching her, he crossed his arms.

"Good morning, Alexander."

"After you've settled in, could you get out the sketches on the cocktail dress you've been working on? I'd like to go over them before the staff meeting."

"Of course."

"Thanks." He smiled at her briefly before turning his attention back to Crystal to give pointers on her sketch.

Nicole nodded at Crystal, who coolly reciprocated, which Nicole suspected was purely for Alexander's benefit. That woman refused to budge an inch in her dislike, and Nicole had long since stopped trying to move her.

She had just retrieved the requested sketches when Alexander walked over and leaned against her desk with his back toward the others in the room. Nicole's desk was pretty isolated. The closest one to her was Monique, and her office was empty presently; thus, they were afforded relative privacy.

"I would have brought the designs to your office, Alexander." She handed him the designs.

"I don't think that's wise." He lowered his voice for her ears only. "It's hard enough keeping my hands off you now. If we were alone in my office…"

"I completely understand."

"I think we should steer clear of each other as much as possible." He pretended interest in the sketches in his hand.

"I agree." She busied her hands with unpacking her portfolio. "Trying not to touch you now is killing me."

"Believe me, I know." His eyes spoke volumes before he cleared his throat and stood. "I'll get back to you on these in a bit."

"I can't wait to hear your thoughts." She forced herself not to watch him leave, instead turning and readying her station for work.

Nicole waited a good fifteen minutes after Alexander returned to his office, so as not to run into him, before going into the break room to get her morning coffee. After her sleepless night, she needed it. What she didn't need was to run into her office enemy.

"Good morning, Crystal." Nicole sighed, walking over to retrieve a cup and saucer from the cupboard.

"I see you're making yourself right at home," Crystal said in an accusing tone.

"What's that supposed to mean?"

"It didn't take you long to move in on the boss."

"First, exactly who would I be moving in on? Alexander isn't dating anyone that I know of. And second—just like you—Alexander and I are business associates." Okay, they were half truths, but she certainly wasn't going to discuss Alexander with Crystal of all people. "I'm flattered that you find me so interesting. However, I'm at a loss to understand why."

"Sure you are." Crystal sneered. "I've worked with women like you before—untalented, unethical and using their bodies to move ahead and get what they want."

"You haven't spent five minutes since I moved here to get to know me, so I don't understand what you're basing your flawed analysis on."

"I have eyes, and I promise you I see very well," Crystal snapped.

"Believe what you want, Crystal. You will anyway." Nicole poured herself a cup of coffee. "I don't have time for high school antics."

"You're so smug," Crystal spat the accusation and fumed when Nicole laughed.

"You're so sad." Nicole's pitying statement caused Crystal's teeth to clench. "What's it to you who Alexander dates? Is it the fact that he's obviously not interested in you that infuriates you so, or are you just the office busybody who isn't happy unless she's stirring up trouble even where none exists?"

"*I* was supposed to work on the Bettina line, but you showed up batting your eyes and wiggling your tail, and lo and behold, suddenly you're assigned to it! Your coup de grâce was talking Alexander into designing a gown with him—a novice like you, designing a gown with the boss! Do you know how many years I've hoped for that honor?"

Nicole studied the other woman and felt a twinge of pity for her. At least she now knew why Crystal disliked her so, even if her reasons were unfounded.

"I—like all of Alexander's employees—follow his orders. If you have a problem with his decisions, I suggest you take it up with him." Without waiting for Crystal's response, she picked up her coffee and walked out.

"If it's the last thing I do, I'm going to find a way to knock you off your high horse!" Crystal angrily promised as she picked up a saucer and smashed it in the sink.

Around 8:00 p.m., after everyone had gone home, Nicole gladly answered a summons into Alexander's office. She found him reclining in his chair behind his desk, jacketless, with a wolfish grin on his face.

"Come here," he ordered.

"Yes, Alexander." She walked over to stand beside his chair. "What can I do for you?"

"Quite a bit." He took her hand and pulled her onto his lap. "I thought everyone would never leave," he groaned against her neck.

"I know." She inhaled his spicy aftershave and ran her hands up and down his chest. "Tell me what you want?"

"I just need one kiss." His mouth sought out hers.

"Just one?" She avoided his lips, smiling.

"Maybe two," he corrected, placing a hand behind her head to bring her mouth in range of his, and nipped at her lower lip. "Or three."

His hot mouth engulfed hers, and she felt singed to the bone. The kiss went on and on, and when they pulled apart, each was breathing raggedly.

"Oh, God, I needed that," he groaned against her mouth.

"Me, too."

He ran fingers down her cheek. "I think I'm good now."

"Well." She smiled sexily, turning until she straddled his lap. "I'm not."

Their mouths mated wildly once more. Her hands made fast work of the buttons of his shirt, and he busied himself unzipping her dress and unhooking her bra.

"I couldn't sleep last night." He murmured against her breasts as his mouth reacquainted itself with her soft skin.

"Neither could I." She gasped as he took a nipple into his mouth. "Don't stop. God, I'm addicted to you."

"I need your sweet mouth."

"Again?" She smiled teasingly.

"Again and again," he growled.

She gave him what he needed, and he kissed her as if this was his last chance. His hands roamed under her skirt to caress her silky inner thighs urgently.

"Let's go back to my place," he suggested against her mouth.

"I'd love to, but first…" She unhooked his belt.

"Nicole…" He groaned at her actions. "We shouldn't do this here."

"Everyone's gone home. There's only you and me." She unbuttoned and unzipped his pants and then stared at him thoughtfully. "Maybe you didn't miss me as much as I missed you?"

"Believe me, I did."

"Then show me how much," she challenged.

"You asked for it." His eyes darkened, and the hands on her thighs moved higher.

"Condom?" She moaned against his mouth and pressed closer as his talented fingers treated her to pleasure.

"Middle drawer," he hoarsely instructed.

She threw the contents on the floor until she found what she was looking for. She held up the foil packet triumphantly before he took it from her, tore it open and quickly sheathed himself.

In the blink of an eye, he was inside of her, filling her, bringing them both to the brink of bliss with each powerful stroke. They desperately tried to make it last, but their need was too great and their passion too explosive. When she began gyrating her hips against his, he lost it, and soon after so did she.

"Mmm." Alex's mouth trailed across her neck and shoulder. "That hit the spot." He raised his head and stared into her satisfied eyes.

Nicole sighed. "It sure did."

"How about coming home with me for more of the same?"

"I'd love to." She lowered her mouth to his. "But first, I just need one more kiss."

Nicole and Alex entered his house laughing and holding hands. She reached up to give him a quick kiss, which turned hot and heavy. Victor came out of the living room and coughed loudly when he spied the kissing couple.

"Hey, guys."

"Hi, Victor." Nicole turned out of Alexander's arms and smiled at him.

"Hey, Vic." Alex wiped lipstick from his mouth until Nicole's fingers took over the job. "What's up?"

"Well, I was hoping for a good meal, but since you're busy…" He slowly walked toward the door.

"Where are you going?" Nicole touched his arm. "I'll whip something up in no time."

"I don't want to intrude."

"Since when?" Alex chuckled. "You know you're more than welcome."

"As long as I'm not in the way."

"You are not," Nicole promised as they all walked to the kitchen. "Let's see what we've got that's quick."

In the kitchen, Nicole and Alex rummaged through the refrigerator and cabinets, pulling out fixings for their impromptu dinner while Victor watched, grinning from the butcher block counter.

They decided on a beef stir fry. Nicole put Victor to

work chopping vegetables and praised his efforts while Alex watched his two favorite people filling his home and heart with laughter.

"Here, make yourself useful." Alex handed a corkscrew to Victor after he finished vegetable patrol.

"I can handle opening wine," Victor assured them, leaving the kitchen for a few moments and going into the wine cellar. He returned with a bottle that he promptly opened flawlessly.

"Beautifully done, Victor," Nicole praised, and he kissed her cheek and handed her a glass. "Thank you."

Alex and Nicole moved around the kitchen seamlessly, as if they'd done it a million times. She handed him spices or utensils before he knew he needed or wanted them, and he volunteered to taste her creation before she asked.

"Are we eating here or the dining room?" Alex asked.

"Here," Nicole and Victor simultaneously agreed and laughed.

"Here it is then," Alex agreed, scooping stir fry onto three plates before sitting beside Nicole at the butcher block.

"Mmm, this hits the spot," Victor said, digging into his food.

"How long has it been since you had a decent meal?" Alex shook his head at his brother.

"When was the last time I was here?" was Victor's response.

"Take the leftovers home with you," Nicole said. "You can reheat, can't you?"

"Barely." Victor chuckled.

Alex watched the two interact with a smile on his face. He loved the way Nicole effortlessly fit in with him and Victor. If he was going to give his heart away, it would be to her. Damn, he wished he wasn't so messed up when it came to trusting because he really wanted to completely trust Nicole.

"Nicole, do you ski?" Victor asked.

"Yes, I do."

"Then you've got to come with me and Alex on our annual ski trip in November."

"That sounds like fun." She glanced at Alexander, who was quiet. "We'll see."

"More wine?" Alex found his voice and refilled everyone's glasses, hoping they would stop the uncomfortable chitchat.

He was aware of Nicole and Victor's curious glances; however, neither of them commented on his sudden less-than-festive mood. An hour later, they all stood by the front door as Victor prepared to leave.

"I hate to eat and run," Victor began.

"Since when?" Alex smiled.

"Want me to stay and help you clean up?"

"No," Alex quickly said. "You're a disaster in the kitchen, and I don't want anything broken."

"I thought not." Victor's eyes danced in amusement. "Now I'm going to leave you two to do some work—or whatever."

"You just couldn't go a few hours without putting your foot in your mouth, could you?" Alex sighed, and Nicole smiled.

"No." Victor laughed, not at all offended. "You guys have fun."

"We will," Alex promised, placing a hand around Nicole's waist.

"That's the spirit." Victor kissed Nicole's cheek. "Thanks for letting me stay for dinner."

"Don't be ridiculous, Victor. This is your home. I'm the one who should be thanking both of you for letting me share part of your lives."

"Boy, do I like you," Victor said. "If my brother messes things up, remember that I'm available."

"He's not going to mess anything up." Nicole laughed, pressing closer to Alexander's side, which she noted was somewhat rigid.

"Good night, Vic," Alex interrupted.

"Don't be jealous, bro. Just be smart and don't let Nicole go," Victor advised, leaving trailing laughter at his brother's deep sigh.

Nicole turned to stare at Alexander's troubled expression. Without saying a word, he walked into the study and she followed him, sitting beside him on the sofa.

"What's wrong, Alexander?"

"Nothing."

"Victor's talking about us being together long-term and my coming along on your ski trip bothered you, didn't it?"

"No, of course not." He stood and walked over to the bar. "How about a nightcap?"

"No, thank you." She walked over to him. "You're upset. Talk to me."

"Nicole." He turned from the bar. "I'm not upset."

"Yes, you are." She refused to be sidetracked. "All the talk tonight about the future upset you. Is it because you don't think we have one together?"

Bingo! He wanted to believe they did, but he didn't.

"I like to live in the present," he slowly admitted. "Is there anything wrong with that?"

"No, but you have to plan ahead sometimes."

"Why?" His innocent question elicited a smile from her.

"Because that's what human beings do—constantly make plans—most of which they never keep. You and Victor schedule a ski trip every year."

"Victor does. I just go along to keep him from nagging me." He shrugged. "Planning is overhyped."

"So you and I never get to make any personal arrangements?" She frowned. "We just live day by day. Is that what you're saying?"

"Nicole, we've got our hands full preparing for our yearly show. Let's concentrate on that," he suggested. He prayed she would drop this because he didn't want to fight with her, and that seemed to be where this was heading.

"Okay." She surprised him by agreeing. "But..."

"Oh, there's a but."

"Yes, there is." She smiled slightly. "When the show's over, we sit down and talk about us—our future."

He stared at her for a long while before agreeing. "Okay."

"Okay," she echoed. Then she kissed him, and after a few seconds he kissed her back. "Now let's go to bed."

"Yeah, let's," he agreed, taking her hand and leading her to the bedroom.

The weeks flew by until it was the end of July. It was hard to believe that in a few weeks the fall fashion show would mark the end of Nicole's six months in Paris, though neither of them discussed her leaving—that is, not until a staff meeting when Alexander took Nicole and everyone else by surprise.

"As you all know, the big fall show is only a few weeks away. I want to thank everyone for their hard work, though it's not over yet." He smiled as groans echoed through the room. "It will be worth it. I do believe this will be one of our best shows ever."

"You're right about that, boss," Monique chimed in.

"This show is going to be extremely special for two reasons. One, it's our first joint endeavor with another house, and second, it marks the end of Nicole's six months with us. We've been very lucky to have her, but after the show, she'll be transferring to our New York office."

Nicole's mouth dropped open at his words, and he avoided looking at her.

"I thought you hadn't decided if you were going back to New York just yet," Monique whispered in her ear.

"I hadn't," she woodenly replied, eyes willing Alexander's to look at her. He eventually did, and the cold look in his eyes sent shivers down her spine. "But I guess I am."

Nicole didn't know what was said for the remainder of the meeting. It was torture having to sit there and act as if everything was fine when she was dying inside. Finally, it was over, and she remained in her seat while everyone filed out.

"Am I such a burden that you can't wait to be rid of me?" she angrily hissed once she and Alexander were alone.

"Nicole." He sighed. "It's not like that."

"No?" Unable to sit down, she jumped up and walked around to the other of the table where he now also stood. "What is it like?"

"You're going to be transferring to the New York office. That was your plan when you came here."

"Plans change, Alexander." She paused and admitted, "You changed my plans."

"What we've had has been good. It's been great, but we both know you're going to be leaving Paris soon, and we need to prepare for that."

"What if I don't want to leave Alexander's Paris office—or you?"

"You're going to, sooner or later."

"What's the matter with you?" She raked angry eyes over him. "Why are you acting like this?"

"I told you I was no good at relationships," Alex said, disquieted by the hurt he saw in her eyes, veiled by anger.

"Alexander, you are relationship material," she softly promised. "We've been in a relationship for months, and it's been great. You know it has. Because you were once hurt by a stupid woman, you think all women are out to do the same thing, but we're not—and I'm definitely not."

"Nicole—"

"How do you feel about me, Alexander?" She gave him one last chance to save her and, more important, himself.

"I care about you," he said.

"You care about me?" He shook his head as she echoed his words. "Alexander, you care about being to work on time, about having food on your table and clothes on your back. How do you *feel* about me?"

"You're important... I don't..." He paused and raked fingers through his hair in frustration. "I don't know what you want me to say."

"I want you to say what's in your heart, but you won't do it, will you?"

"Why can't we just keep things the way they are and enjoy the time we have left?"

"Why do you insist on limiting us?" Her eyes begged for understanding.

"Because that's the way it is." His unsatisfactory response appalled her.

"I'd better get back to work."

He grabbed her arm, fingers tightening when she tried to pull away. "Nicole, let's not—"

"Take your hand off me, Alexander." Her voice was soft but serious.

He stared at her for a few tense seconds before doing as she asked. She left and forced herself to show no emotion as she returned to her station. She'd make it through this miserable day if it killed her.

Alexander sat back down and cradled his head in his hands. He wanted to call Nicole back and tell her what she wanted and deserved to hear—that he loved being with her—but after the show she'd be gone. He had to keep reminding himself of that. What he had just done was for the best.

Why, then, did he feel so miserable?

Chapter 16

Alex stared out the bedroom window into the night as he held an untouched glass of bourbon. Alcohol couldn't dull the ache encompassing his heart. It was 3:00 a.m., and he hadn't been able to sleep at all. A hundred times he started to call Nicole, but what would he say?

The doorbell rang, and he wanted to ignore it, but after the insistent ringing he relented. Who the hell was at his door at this hour? Maybe it was Victor stopping by after a night on the town, as he was known to do occasionally.

"All right, I'm coming!" He stalked from his bedroom in bare feet and bare chest, wearing only black pajama bottoms, and opened the door.

"Nicole." He was shocked.

"May I come in?"

"Of course." He stepped aside and she entered, removing her jean jacket and tossing it over a nearby chair.

"I know this is an indecent hour to visit, but I couldn't sleep."

"I couldn't either." He ushered her into the living room.

"I am so angry with you," she softly confessed when they were seated on the sofa.

"I know, and I deserve it." He fought against touching her, not certain how she would react if he did. "I'm a mess, Nicole. You deserve better."

"Maybe I think you're the best." She paused, allowing her soft words to sink in. "Did you ever think of that?"

"How could you?"

"Because you are." She softly touched his cheek. "Open up to me. Tell me why you're trying so hard to push me away. I don't think this is about Nina, is it?"

He sighed. "No."

"Was there someone else?" She squeezed his hand. "Tell me what you're feeling. Talk to me, please."

He was silent, thinking. Finally he turned to face her again and sat down beside her.

"My parents were married for thirty-five years. Ten of them were happy. Ten out of thirty-five." He shook his head in disgust. "I guess they were in love once, but their marriage soured quickly, and that—along with my own failed relationship—is all the proof I need that love doesn't last."

"My parents have been together for thirty-nine happy years, so I'm here to tell you true love does last. Alexander, the past shapes us. There's no way around that, but we don't have to let it define us."

"How can I not? Victor and I lived through years of our parents deliberately doing everything they could to hurt each other. We watched their marriage disintegrate into a loveless, hateful nightmare. Thank God we had tutors and nannies, or I don't know what would have become of us." He paused before continuing, as if a dam had burst within him. "Neither would grant the other a divorce. They lived to make each other's lives miserable. They had countless affairs and didn't care how it affected me and Victor. I vowed I would do better than they did, but I got involved with Nina—a disastrous encounter that almost ruined my reputation and destroyed my company. So it turns out I was just as pathetic at maintaining a healthy relationship as they were. I promised myself I wasn't going to let anyone in ever again."

"Alexander..." At his name on her lips, his eyes grew tender.

"Then I met you."

"And you felt vulnerable all over again."

"Yeah, and I don't like it."

"Given your history, I understand."

He was shocked at her statement. "Do you?"

"Of course I do. It's hard for you to trust because you don't have any positive examples to go by. God, given the childhood you described, I can't blame you for feeling that way."

She never did what he expected. He didn't think he would ever have a civil conversation with her again after their fight today.

"You're special, Nicole. I shouldn't have announced to the office that you were leaving without talking to you first. I was just—"

"Just trying to protect yourself from the inevitable."

"Yes."

"One thing you can count on, Alexander." She cupped his cheek in her palm. "If and when I'm ready to say goodbye to you, I'll say it to your face. All right?"

He smiled. "All right."

"I love you, Alexander. You don't have to say anything. I just want you to know how I feel so that maybe you'll believe me when I say I'm not walking away from you." She stared deeply into his conflicted eyes. "You have to decide what you want."

Part of him was happy by her admission, and another was saddened. Love didn't last; that he knew firsthand.

"I want you," he finally admitted. He didn't believe they had a future together, but he did want her.

"Here I am." She opened her arms wide, and he pulled her close. "Believe in us, Alexander," she pleaded.

"I want to."

"I'll help you," she promised. "We're meant to be," she whispered in his ear. "Happily ever after does exist. You'll see."

He held her close, glad she couldn't see his worried expression. He wanted to believe her, wanted to think they would last, but happy endings didn't seem to exist for him—and he doubted they ever would.

The big night of Alexander's fall fashion show was finally upon them. Nicole and Monique were putting the finishing touches on their makeup when their doorbell rang. They met each other in the hallway, and Nicole opened the door to admit Victor.

"Victor, hi." Nicole gave him a hug. "Where's Alexander? Parking the car?"

"No." Victor rolled his eyes in disgust. "He's still at the office working on some secret project."

"The show starts in an hour and a half. We're going to be late!"

"I tried to tell him that." Victor shook his head and sighed. "Why don't you go to the office and pry him away?"

"Me?" Nicole pointed to herself. "If you couldn't do it, I can't."

"Have you looked at yourself in the mirror?" He appreciatively eyed the red chiffon halter dress that flowed as she walked. Her back was completely bare, as were her shoulders and arms. The bodice was geometrically cut, showing peeks of brown skin. The long skirt stopped just above her ankles, leading to red strappy high-heeled shoes. Her hair was arranged in soft curls with bangs and wispy strands flirting with her eyes. "One look at you and he'll forget all about work."

"Thank you."

"He keeps a tux in the office because he's always working," Victor said. "Go and get him, or the evening will be a disaster."

"Okay, I'll give it a try." Nicole grabbed her matching wrap and evening bag and walked out.

About twenty minutes later, Nicole entered Alexander's office and found him bent over his desk working, as Victor has foretold. She shook her head, smiled and walked in.

Without looking up he said, "Dammit Vic, I told you I'll be one…" His voice trailed off when he glanced up and saw Nicole. "Wow."

"You approve?" Nicole twirled around slowly to give him the full effect before walking over to sit on his lap.

"And how…" Appreciative eyes roamed over her, along with just as appreciative hands.

"I thought you were going to stand me up." She sighed as his lips settled in the crook of her neck.

"I'm sorry, I was just engrossed."

She glanced at his designs. "These are wonderful. Are they for a new collection?"

"Yep. Inspiration just hit me a day ago. You're the only one who's seen them."

"I can't wait to see the final versions." Nicole thumbed through the sketches as Alexander's lips traversed her shoulders and back until she turned and encircled his neck with her arms. "I know it's hard to break the artistic flow, but we've got to get going."

He glanced regretfully at his designs. She knew that

look and the feelings behind it well; she'd had them often enough herself.

"They will be here in the morning," she promised, caressing his cheek. "How many times have you told me that?"

"I know, but—"

"No buts." She shook her head, and he sighed in resignation. "Tonight we play, and tomorrow we work."

"Okay." They both stood, and he pulled her into his arms and kissed her thoroughly. As usual when they touched, desire erupted. When she felt his hands working on the side zip of her dress, she pushed out of his arms.

"Uh-uh."

"Why not?" He purposefully approached her with decadent desire written in his eyes, which she found almost impossible to resist.

She held up a hand to ward him off. "Because we have a fashion show to attend."

"Let's blow it off." He grabbed her hand and pulled her into his arms.

"You're one of the hosts," she said, avoiding his lips, which landed on her cheek. "You can't forget about it."

He sighed against her ear. "I hate parties."

"We'll have one of our own later," she promised.

He raised his head and smiled expectantly. "Yeah?"

"Definitely." She kissed his lips softly. "But first, go and get changed into your tux."

"Okay." He took a key out of his pocket and handed it to her. "Will you lock the designs away for me in the center drawer?"

"Will do." She gathered his designs. "Hurry up. We don't want to be late." She smiled at his pained expression and locked his designs in his desk as he requested.

Alexander and Nicole made it to the fashion show right on time, and it went off without a hitch. They were mingling at the after-party when Nicole felt him visibly tense. She glanced at him, but he was staring straight ahead, jaw clenched in displeasure.

"Alexander, what's wrong?" He didn't answer her. She followed his gaze and encountered a tall, model-like brunette, who was staring right back at Alexander. Instinctively, Nicole knew she must be Nina Laurent. She grabbed a flute of champagne from a passing waiter and began walking toward them.

"Hello, Alex. It's been a long time." Nina smiled. At his continued silence she asked, "Aren't you going to introduce me to your date?"

"No." Alex barked the syllable and turned to leave, but Nina touched his arm, which he immediately snatched away.

She smiled and extended a hand in Nicole's direction. "I'm Nina Laurent, Alex's ex-designer—among other things."

"Nice to meet you," Nicole lied as she briefly shook the other woman's hand.

"And your name?"

"Nicole."

"So you're the new employee."

"You've heard of me? I wish I could say the same of you."

Nina's eyes shot daggers at Nicole's carefully aimed barb.

"A word of advice, dear. Watch out for big bad Alex. He eats little girls like you for breakfast."

"I'm not a little girl, and whatever plans Alexander and I have are our own concern," Nicole smoothly responded and was satisfied when the other woman's smile was replaced with an angry sneer.

"I would say it was nice to see you again, Nina, but I'd

be lying," Alex interjected, guiding Nicole away, leaving Nina glaring after them.

"She's a lovely woman," Nicole said with such sarcasm that Alex laughed out loud and impulsively pulled her close to his side.

"You handled her beautifully. I wish I knew who invited her."

"It doesn't matter." She draped her arm in his. "Forget about her and concentrate on me."

"That won't be hard to do." He smiled at her. "How about some champagne?"

"I'd love some."

"I'll be right back," he promised, squeezing her hand as he walked off to find a waiter.

While she waited for Alex, Nicole was shocked and giddy as Felipe Varcellegao came up to talk to her. She didn't know if she'd ever get used to being in the same room with the biggest names in fashion.

"Felipe Varcellegao seems taken with your little toy." Nina intercepted Alex as he was headed back to Nicole's side.

"We have nothing to say to one another, Nina."

"She seems very chummy with your competition." Nina continued to block his way. "Doesn't she?"

Alex glanced over her shoulder and fought off a frown. "They're just talking."

"That's how it starts." Nina sipped her champagne. "Isn't it?"

"Not everyone has your lack of loyalty or back alley ethics."

"My my, you've sharpened your barbs, haven't you?"

"They're not barbs. They're the truth."

"If your precious Nicole is happy with Alexander's and you, why is she taking Felipe's business card?" Alex's eyes shot back to Nicole as she placed a white card in her evening bag. "Maybe there's trouble in paradise after all."

"I don't know what I ever saw in you," Alex snarled and walked off. Thankfully when he reached Nicole, she was alone. "I saw you talking with Felipe." He handed her a glass. "What was that about?"

"Nothing." She sipped her champagne. "He was just congratulating Alexander's on a fabulous show."

"That's nice." He pushed all doubts out of his head. Nina was a troublemaker, and he wouldn't allow her to ruin his and Nicole's evening. "May I have this dance?"

"I thought you'd never ask." She took his hand and walked with him onto the dance floor. Soon they were surrounded by other dancers, and neither of them noticed Nina positioning herself within hearing distance.

"Alexander...?" She paused, thinking better of her unspoken question.

"What?" She shook her head, but he persisted. "What is it, Nicole?"

"I just wondered if you wanted to talk about Nina."

"No," he quickly said. "Suffice it to say that woman was my worst nightmare, and I'm glad to be rid of her."

"I'm so sorry she hurt you. I don't understand how anyone with a soul could ever hurt you." His heart somersaulted at her genuine words.

"I think you're a little prejudiced."

"I am completely," she vowed.

"I've never been happier than I have been with you, Nicole." He didn't know what the future held, but he wanted her to know.

"We're just getting started." At his silence, she asked, "Do you believe me?"

"I want to."

"Then do," she softly ordered, and he smiled.

"What do you say we swing by the office on the way home?" He purposefully switched subjects.

"Alexander." Nicole shook her head tolerantly. "Tonight is for play, remember?"

"I know, but ideas for my new designs are dancing in my head. You know what that's like."

"I do." She lowered her voice, "But you promised me the rest of the night, and I'm very selfish when it comes to my private time with you."

A pleased smile lit up his face. "Is that right?"

"Yes." She fought down the urge to kiss him, and when his eyes shifted to her lips she knew he was fighting the same battle. "How much longer should we stay here?"

"At least an hour." He chuckled at her groan. "Let's go and mingle and see if we can't speed up our timetable."

"What a wonderful idea." She touched his arm and moved closer, whispering, "Then I want to go home and have our own private party, lover."

"Make that thirty minutes," Alexander growled.

"Better and better." She squeezed his fingers as they left the dance floor.

"Hi, Gus. Know who this is?" Nina used her sexiest voice for this important call as she exited the boring party. She listened and laughed seductively. "I know, it's been too long, baby. That's why I'm calling. Are you at work? Perfect! Hang on a second." She gave the attendant her claim ticket and walked outside to wait for her car and to continue her conversation in private. "How would you like to make a quick twenty grand? All you have to do is unlock a door. Yep, that's all. I'll give you the details when I get there. See you soon, baby."

She pressed a button to end the call and waited impatiently for her car. She couldn't wait to create a little trouble in paradise. Nothing made her happier.

* * *

"I am glad to be home," Alex proclaimed as he and Nicole entered his bedroom.

"Me, too." Nicole sighed. "It was quite a night, wasn't it?"

"I hope it's not over with yet." Alex's arms snaked around her waist, pulling her tight.

"It's just beginning for us," Nicole promised, pushing him onto the bed and following him down.

Their lips gravitated together and they kissed reverently, drawing each other into the waiting vortex. Their hands made quick work of divesting each other of their clothes, and then they showed how much they cherished each other. Their breath intermingled in satisfied sighs, limbs intertwined in perfect synchronization as two hearts and minds blended seamlessly into one before the excruciating pleasure built inside of them until all they could do was pray for sweet release.

"Oh, God, Nicole!"

"Alexander!"

The world exploded, showering them with the white-hot sparks of fulfillment from their culminated passion. When they had finally come back down to earth long minutes later, they basked in the sweet afterglow, constantly touching.

"I can't imagine my life without you, Nicole."

Her heart contracted happily at his unsolicited admission. She slid up his body until they were at eye level with each other.

"I'm so glad I have you."

"You do have me—forever, Alexander. I love you." She sealed her promise with a sweetly tender, lingering kiss that she was certain made him believe her—if only for a little while.

Chapter 17

After a most romantic night, Nicole entered Alexander's on cloud nine. She was certain she and Alexander were on the verge of making a long-lasting commitment. He had dropped her off at her apartment earlier to change and then went on to work. As she exited the elevator, the happy smile on her face fell quickly as she witnessed the unusual chaos in the office. People were milling about or huddled together talking animatedly among themselves.

"Nicole, I need to speak with you." Alexander appeared out of nowhere and took her hand. "Let's go to my office."

She followed him, and once they reached the seclusion of his office, she touched his rigid arm. "Alexander, what's wrong?"

"My designs were stolen last night."

She gasped. "Which ones?"

"For the new line." He paused before pointedly adding, "The ones I only showed you."

"How could they be stolen?"

"That's what I'm trying to find out. Everyone's work-station is being searched as we speak."

"You don't think it was anyone working here, do you?"

He ran fingers through his hair. "I don't know what to think."

"Alexander…" The way he was looking at her halted her words.

"I need to search your station, Nicole."

Her mouth dropped open at his cool statement. She tried to convince herself that his request was routine; everyone's station was being searched, and though he knew she was innocent, he had to search hers for appearance's sake.

"All right."

"Let's go." He followed her out. She didn't know why she felt such dread as they walked to her desk; she hadn't stolen his designs, so they wouldn't be found there. But she still had a sinking feeling in the pit of her stomach.

"I'm sorry about this, Nicole," Monique said.

"No, I understand." She spoke the words, but she had no understanding of this distasteful situation at all.

Nicole unlocked her desk and stood back while Monique and Alexander emptied the contents onto the desk top. She gasped when Monique pulled out a large envelope addressed to the competitor she had been chatting with at the party last night.

"What's this, Nicole?" Alexander picked up the envelope and showed it to her.

"I—I don't know."

He opened the envelope, and she knew from the clenching of his fingers crushing the paper what was inside.

"These are my designs." Alexander's voice was strained. "The envelope is addressed to Felipe Varcellegao, whom you were speaking with last night."

Her voice caught in her throat as she whispered, "What are you implying?"

"I'm just stating a fact. How did my designs get in your desk, Nicole?"

"How should I know?" She placed a hand to her aching head. "Alexander, you know I didn't do this." At his deafening silence she asked, "Don't you?"

"I don't know what to believe."

"You don't know what to believe?" She whispered in shock. "You actually think that I…" She was unable to finish that distasteful sentence. "How could you think that of me?" Without waiting for him to respond she continued, "When did I have time to steal your designs? I've been with you constantly until you dropped me off at home this morning."

"I don't know," he admitted. "I don't know anything anymore, except that my designs were in your desk."

"But I didn't put them there!" She gathered her purse and slung it on her shoulder. "You should *know* that!"

"Where are you going?"

"Home."

"We're not finished here, Nicole."

"I'm *definitely* finished here. If you want to stop me, call security!" She stalked off past curious, shocked eyes, including the gloating ones of Crystal.

"Did you have anything to do with this?" Nicole stopped long enough to confront Crystal.

"I don't know what you're talking about."

"Sure you don't." Nicole continued on her way. It didn't matter if Crystal had set her up or not—the important thing was Alexander's complete lack of trust in her, and she couldn't blame anyone for that except him.

Monique shot Alexander a murderous look before running after Nicole. She caught up with her at the elevator and placed a comforting arm around her shoulders.

"Good morning, ladies." Victor's greeting to Monique and Nicole wasn't reciprocated as they entered the elevator.

* * *

Victor frowned as Alex approached him. "All right, bro. I'm here at this ungodly hour. What in the world is going on?"

"In my office, Vic." Alexander walked off with his brother following. His head was spinning, and his stomach was tied up in knots. He didn't want to believe the worst of Nicole, but what was he supposed to think? He felt like a magnet for deception. "Alexander's was robbed last night."

"What? How?" Victor listened as Alex related the events of the past twelve hours.

"Alex, you didn't accuse Nicole, did you?"

"No, I simply asked her—"

"Oh, brother!" Victor sighed in disgust. "No wonder she looked about ready to kill someone."

"I had every right—" Alex began, and Victor's upheld hand silenced his angry tirade.

"You were wrong, and you know it," Victor softly interrupted, his quiet definitive tone taking all fight out of his brother. "There are other, much more plausible culprits than Nicole."

"I considered Nina or even Crystal, but no one knew about my new designs except Nicole." Alex felt sick saying that. He didn't want to believe Nicole would do this to him—not Nicole.

"Have you never heard of a setup?"

"The designs were in Nicole's desk, Vic, and she was the only one who knew where I kept them."

"I still put my money on Nina. She didn't like being dismissed by you, personally or professionally," Victor said.

"How did she know about my designs?" Alex asked. "More important, how could she have gotten past security?"

"Please, we're talking about Nina—whomever she had

to sleep with or bribe to get what she wanted, that's what she did," Victor said as Alex snatched up the phone.

"This is the second call I've made, and I assure you it will be the last before I replace the lot of you," he warned. "I want all security personnel in my office in five minutes. Everyone!" He slammed down the phone.

Victor took out his laptop. "Let me run my security program to check the PCs."

"What good will that do?" Alex paced in front of his desk.

"A bonus of my new software is a built-in security program that utilizes hidden cameras and runs constantly, which is why I was adamant the monitors had to remain on standby at all times. Only I can access the program."

Alex stilled and frowned. "You never mentioned that before."

"I had a few bugs to work out first—and you know what a perfectionist you are."

"Check it out and let me know what you find."

"We already know what I'll find."

"Damn!" The knot in his stomach moved to his throat, almost choking him. He needed to talk to Nicole. He thought about calling her, but she probably wouldn't answer. He'd go in person as soon as he could.

"You should call Nicole." Victor read his mind.

"Once I get to the bottom of this." Had he been wrong not to trust Nicole?

The security team arrived, and Alex interrogated all of them except Gus, the one who had been on duty last night. The head of security was on his way to Gus's house. Minute by minute, the knot in Alex's stomach grew bigger. When Victor glanced up from his computer screen, the look on his face said it all.

"Well, what did you find?" Alex asked.

"Just what I expected to find." Victor set his notebook down in front of Alex and pressed a few keys. "Here's the security footage Gus thought he erased."

They watched the screen, and Alex's fist clenched when Nina was let into Alexander's by Gus. She handed him a fat envelope full of cash and received a key in return. Once in Alex's office, she used the key to unlock Alex's desk and found his designs shortly thereafter. Then she went into the designer's area and searched until she found Nicole's desk, where she planted the stolen sketches .

"Dammit!" Alex's fist smashed on his desk.

"Go," Victor ordered. "You'd better make it the best apology you've ever given."

"I'll try." Alex looked forlorn. "I don't know if any apology is going to be enough."

"You can do it." Victor slapped him on the shoulder for encouragement. "Nicole's the best thing that's ever happened to you, Alex. Go and tell her you're sorry. She'll forgive you."

Alex wasn't so sure, but he knew he had to try.

"I hope you're right." He walked toward the door but stopped and turned to glance at his brother. "Thanks, Vic. I owe you."

"You owe me nothing…but…" Victor smiled. "Does that mean I can borrow the Ferrari?"

"Wouldn't it be simpler to just buy one of your own?"

"Why spend all that money when I can borrow my loving brother's?"

Alex laughed, fished in his pocket and took the Ferrari key off his key ring and tossed it to his brother. "You earned it."

Victor kissed the key, then said, "Let me drop you off at Nicole's. I don't want you in a cab again."

"Thanks." Alex managed a small smile as they walked out.

* * *

Alex stood on Nicole's threshold, praying Monique wasn't home so they could speak privately. He had some major apologizing to do, and he'd rather do it without an audience. He tapped his foot impatiently and knocked for the third time. Finally, the door opened, and Nicole glared unwelcomingly at him.

"What do you want?"

"Nicole." He sighed her name. "May I come in?"

"No."

"Please." He stared into her eyes, easily recognizing the hurt beneath the anger. "I know I hurt you. I was wrong. Please let me explain."

She relented. "Say your piece and leave." He followed her into the apartment, and she turned to face him. "I'm waiting."

"I know you had nothing to do with stealing my designs."

"What changed your mind?" Her frown increased when he hesitated in answering her.

"I saw the security footage. Nina bribed one of the guards at the office to let her in last night."

"Let me get this straight." She smiled humorlessly. "You're sorry because you found proof of my innocence— not because you *knew* in your heart that I was innocent? Is that right?"

"Nicole…"

"Is that supposed to make me feel better?" He remained silent, and she angrily continued, "How could you think I would *ever* betray you, Alexander?"

"I didn't want to."

"But you did!" She balled her fists at her sides. "I deserved better than that!"

"Yes, you did—you do," he quickly agreed.

"You could have given me better. You could have given

me everything." Her voice trembled slightly. "All you had to do was trust me. After all we've been to each other, have I ever given you any reason to doubt my love or loyalty?"

"No, you haven't." He was losing her; he felt her slipping away with each word spoken.

"No," she repeated sarcastically. "Alexander, we were as close as two people can get. How could you not trust *me?*" Her eyes begged for understanding.

"I wanted to trust you. I tried, I really did, and as much as I'm capable, I do trust you."

"How can you say that?" She shook her head in disbelief. "You don't accuse someone you trust of theft and betrayal. Those three things are not synonymous."

"You're aware of my history with Nina and my parents."

"I am not them, Alexander, and I'm tired of you comparing me to other people!" He could tell she meant every word, and icy cold fingers of fear gripped his heart. "I want to be judged for who I am and what I've done. Is that too much to ask?"

"No, it's not."

"Then why couldn't you do that?"

"I should have."

"Yes, you should have," she agreed, opening the door for him. "I'd like you to leave now."

"Nicole—"

"Goodbye, Alexander," she sharply cut him off.

He wanted to say more but left as she asked. Had he known how final her words would turn out to be, he would have stayed and talked himself blue trying to convince her of the sincerity of his apology.

Nicole wiped away a tear from her cheek and leaned against the door as her heart broke into a million pieces. She would not cry; she would purge her love for Alexander from her soul—somehow. She laughed bitterly. Who was she kidding? She might as well try to stop breathing than try to stop loving him—but that love was useless. They had no future because he didn't trust her. He didn't even know what the word meant, and without trust, there could be no love.

Nicole didn't come in the next day and wouldn't return his calls, and he couldn't blame her. He called Monique into his office.

"How's Nicole?" Alex motioned for her to sit down, but she defiantly remained standing.

"Do you really care?"

"Of course I care. What kind of question is that?"

"After you broke her heart by accusing her of stealing from you and betraying your trust, I'd say it's a fair question."

"Where is she, Monique?"

"Why? So you can hurt her some more?" At his pained expression, she glanced at her watch. "About now, she should be touching down."

"Touching down?" He leaned forward in his chair. "Where is she?"

"New York." Monique walked out before he could say anything else.

Alex sank back onto his chair, utter disbelief and shock evident on his face. Nicole was gone? She had left him? Now what was he going to do?

Alex spent the rest of the day telling himself it was for the best that he and Nicole were over and that he really didn't miss her and definitely didn't need her. A funny thing happened in the midst of trying to convince himself of those lies, though—he found the truth. Despite his resolve not to, he had fallen head over heels in love with Nicole. He wanted and needed her back in his life, but

would she have him? There was only one thing to do—
go and find out.

He now sat on his private plane bound for New York.
He was going to do whatever he had to do to get her back.
He forced the nagging possibility that she wouldn't forgive him to the back of his mind. She loved him and he
loved her; they would work this out. She'd forgive him.
She had to because he honestly didn't know what he'd do
if she didn't.

Picking up the phone, he dialed his brother's number.
"Hey, Vic, it's me. Can you look after Alexander's for a
few days or a week—maybe longer?"

"Sure I can, but where will you be?"

"In New York."

"Yes!" Alex managed a smile at Victor's exuberance.
"Bring your lady back, bro."

"I'm going to give it everything I have," he solemnly
promised.

"You'll succeed." Alex envied Victor's certainty. "I have
faith in you."

"Thanks, Vic."

"*De nada,* bro. Now get off the phone and get going."

"I'm already on my plane. Talk to you later, Vic."

"Bye, bro. Good luck."

As he rang off, he prayed for a miracle. He had a feeling he was going to need one.

Chapter 18

Nicole walked through the front door of her parents' house without being seen. She had been back in New York since last night and had taken a little time to pull herself together before coming home. She stood unobserved in the hall, watching her family with envy.

Natasha and Damien sat side by side on a sofa to the left of the fireplace. His arm was around her shoulders, his other resting on her protuberant stomach. Nicole smiled genuinely for the first time in days. At least she hadn't missed the birth; Natasha was a few days late and was scheduled for induction next week if she hadn't delivered by then.

Nathan sat on the opposite sofa with Marcy. He was running his fingers absently through her hair. She turned to smile at him, and he placed a light kiss on her lips before pulling her head down onto his shoulder, his fingers still entwined in her hair.

Her mother and Marcy and Damien's mother entered

from the kitchen, presumably after checking on dinner, chatting happily before sitting down beside their respective husbands, who were engaged in a game of chess.

They all fit together. They were so perfect for each other. Why couldn't she find what they had? She had, she sadly reminded herself, but she couldn't force Alexander to realize they were meant to be together. Though he had hurt her terribly, buried deep among the hurt of her tattered heart, she still believed they belonged together. If only he did, too.

"Hi, everyone!" She made her voice appropriately light, hoping she could convince her family she was as happy as she had been when she had left them six months ago.

"Nicole!" Natasha exclaimed as she stood with Damien's help and walked toward her.

"Tash, how are you?" Nicole touched her huge stomach.

"Ready for my darling baby to make an entrance." Natasha groaned, and everyone laughed.

"He was just waiting for his aunt to come home," Nicole said.

"I hope so." Natasha rubbed her stomach. "Your aunt Nicole has returned. Now it's time for you to come out."

Damien hid a smile behind his hand and kissed his very pregnant wife's cheek. "Why didn't you tell us you were coming?" he asked Nicole.

"That's Nicole for you—always doing the unexpected," Nathan said.

"My baby is home!" her mother exclaimed, hugging her tightly. Then her father enveloped her in his strong arms.

"What's wrong, Nicole?" Her mother inspected her artificial smile. "And don't try to tell me it's nothing. I'm your mother," Linda chided.

"I'm fine, Momma, really."

"This sadness in your eyes is the work of a man," Linda correctly deduced. "Isn't it?"

Nicole remained noticeably silent. She wasn't ready to talk about Alexander; the wounds were too fresh and the pain too sharp.

"You look wonderful, Nicole." Marcy intervened. "Now, the most important question is did you do a lot of shopping, and what did you bring us?" Everyone laughed and looked at Nicole expectantly.

Nicole gave Marcy a grateful smile for changing the subject. She hoped everyone would take her lead, which thankfully they did, at least for now.

"Yes I did do some shopping, and I have something for everyone." She laughed as the room erupted in cheers.

The doorbell chimed, and because she was still standing and nearest to the door, Natasha went to answer it.

"Yes, may I help you?"

"You must be Natasha." Alexander smiled, recognizing her from the photos Nicole kept on her desk.

"I am, and you are?"

"I'm Alexander James. I worked with Nicole in Paris. Is Nicole here?"

"Yes, she is."

"May I come in?"

"I'm considering it." Natasha studied him coolly for a few seconds longer before stepping aside.

"May I see Nicole?" he asked anxiously as he removed his jacket.

"I don't know if she wants to see you."

"Please, I've come a long way, and it's urgent that I talk to her."

Again he was treated to intense scrutiny while she considered his request. After what seemed like hours, she came to a decision.

"She's in the living room." She motioned for him to follow her. "This way."

All talking and laughing ceased when Natasha and Alexander entered the room. Everyone stared at him questioningly.

Nicole's mouth dropped open in shock as she slowly rose to her feet and walked over to the man she was trying to purge from her heart. "What are you doing here, Alexander?"

"I came to talk to you."

"We said it all in Paris." She silently cursed her heart for nearly jumping out of her chest at the sight of him. From somewhere deep inside, a flicker of hope sprang to life. He had come all this way for her. He must have left Paris shortly after she did. The fact that he had dropped everything touched her; however, it all depended on what he said and did next.

"Can I talk to you alone?" He glanced at the occupants of the room, who glared back at him.

"No. If you want to talk to me, talk."

Every pair of hostile eyes in the room rested on him. He recognized them all from the pictures on Nicole's desk, but they had looked much friendlier on paper than they did now. This was too important for him to mess up, so he sighed before forcing himself to focus only on her instead of the stares sent his direction from her family.

"I'm sorry for hurting you, Nicole," he began. "I'm so sorry for the things I did and didn't say."

"You think saying you're sorry makes up for everything, don't you?"

"No, but I am sorry."

"Too little, too late, Alexander." She wasn't giving an inch until she heard the one thing that would convince her of his sincerity.

"I don't believe that."

"What exactly do you believe?" Her eyes burned angrily. "Do you still believe I'm a thief and a liar?"

"I never said that." He shifted uncomfortably as the unfriendly stares were now laced with outrage.

"You didn't?" A perfectly arched eyebrow rose. "The man accusing me of stealing his precious designs looked so much like you."

"Nicole, I—"

"Knowing how I felt about you, how could you entertain for a second that I would *ever* betray you?" Without giving him a chance to answer, she continued, "Every time I tried to show you what true love was, you threw it back in my face."

"I know. All I can say in my defense is that I'm used to being hurt, and for self-preservation's sake, I couldn't let you all the way into my heart. But you got in anyway, Nicole, and I'm glad you did."

"Well, I'm not," she whispered. "No one has ever hurt me the way you did."

"I know I did." His hand reached for her, but her angry expression stopped him from touching her. She wanted to feel his arms around her, his lips on hers, but she wasn't going to forgive him for not trusting her—not until he said the words she longed to hear. "Nicole, I never had anyone love me the way you do. I didn't even know that type of love existed. I didn't know how to handle such devotion and selflessness."

"I gave you everything I had to give. I laid my heart open for you, and you trampled on it."

"If I could go back and change things—if I could take away the pain I caused you, the one person I never wanted to hurt—I would do it in a heartbeat. When I found out you had left Paris, I'd never been more scared in my life because I finally realized I don't have a life without you."

She felt herself weakening, but refused to give in to her love for him until he realized what he put her through.

"Just words, Alexander."

"No, not just words. For once I'm being completely honest with myself, and especially with you. God, Nicole, I don't know what else to say except that I love you." He spoke the words she had waited so long to hear. "I love you with my heart and my soul and with everything that I am. I didn't believe in us, and I'm sorry. I don't deserve it, but if you give me another chance, I promise I'll spend the rest of my life trying to make it up to you."

He waited for her to speak, but she could only stare at him with tears welling in her eyes. He had finally said the one thing that would allow her to forgive him—he loved her. She was paralyzed with joy.

"Nicole, love hurts sometimes, but that's just love," Natasha promised. "Give Alex another chance."

"Listen to your sister, Nicole," her mother chimed in. "Her words are wise and true."

"Give the man a break, sis," Nathan suggested, patting Alex on the shoulder comfortingly. "After all, he came all this way and faced down your entire family, didn't he?"

"Yes, you pigheaded men do like to stick together, don't you?" Marcy screwed up her nose at her husband and laughed when he encircled her waist and kissed her before pulling her into the dining room.

"I don't think we could have done better ourselves, Linda," Margaret Johnson whispered.

"He does seem like a nice man," Linda agreed as they headed out of the room. Their husbands trailed behind them, shaking their heads. Damien and Natasha followed.

"Maybe I will forgive you," Nicole said finally.

Once they were alone, Alex took her hand in his, led her to the sofa and waited until she sat down before kneeling in front of her, still holding her hand. He took a midnight blue velvet box out of his left jacket pocket and opened it, revealing a princess-cut diamond solitaire engagement ring.

"I love you, Nicole. You taught me to love. You breathed life into my cold heart, and I'm so sorry for trampling on your trust and your love. I would understand if you throw this ring back in my face, but please don't." Taking the ring from its bed, he slipped it onto her finger slowly. "Marry me."

She lowered to the floor until she was kneeling in front of him. She took his face between her hands; the look in her eyes gave him her answer.

"What took you so long to ask?" she whispered through tears.

He smiled ruefully. "I was a fool."

"Yes, you were, but a fool I've always loved."

"Will you marry me?" he asked again, needing to hear the words from her.

"Yes." She ended his torment, pulling his lips to hers.

"Nicole, I thought I'd lost you," he brokenly confessed, crushing her to him. "Thank God I didn't."

"I'll love you forever, Alexander."

They kissed, tentatively at first, as if neither could believe they were actually together again, and then with increasing fervor when the passion between them erupted as it always did when they touched. When he tried to end the kiss, she wound her arms around his neck, prolonging contact for innumerably pleasing seconds.

"Just don't try to live without me again," she warned.

"I don't have a life without you. You own my heart, Nicole."

"And I plan on keeping it," she whispered into his mouth.

"Hey, you two, come on. Dinner is going to get cold!" Nathan shouted from the dining room.

"Nathan, leave them alone," Marcy scolded.

"Dinner is going to get cold," Alex reiterated against Nicole's lips as her arms tightened around his neck.

"Let it," Nicole whispered and pulled his mouth back to hers as they shared the sweetest embrace either had ever known.

* * * * *

A sizzling new miniseries set in the wide-open spaces of Montana!

THE BROWARDS OF MONTANA
Passionate love in the West

JACQUELIN THOMAS	DARA GIRARD	HARMONY EVANS

WRANGLING WES	**ENGAGING BROOKE**	**LOVING LANEY**
Available April 2014	*Available May 2014*	*Available June 2014*

REQUEST YOUR FREE BOOKS!

2 FREE NOVELS
PLUS 2 FREE GIFTS!

KIMANI™ ROMANCE

Love's ultimate destination!